Ain't Goin' to Glory

Ain't Goin' to Glory

DAVID
DELMAN

St. Martin's Press
New York

Acknowledgment
The majority of illustrations in this book are from various editions of
Harper's Weekly and *Leslie's Illustrated Weekly* of 1863. The publisher is
grateful to the source of these and other illustrations of the period, the
New York Public Library Picture Collection and the New York Public
Library Research Division.

DESIGN BY DAWN NILES

Library of Congress Cataloging-in-Publication Data

Delman, David.
    Ain't goin' to glory / David Delman.
        p.   cm.
    "A Thomas Dunne book."
    ISBN 0-312-06272-9
    1. Draft Riot, New York, N.Y., 1863—Fiction. 2. New York (N.Y.)
—History—Civil War, 1861–1865—Fiction. I. Title.
    PS3554.E444A74   1991
    813'.54—dc20   91-20933
                                                                         CIP

First Edition: September 1991
10 9 8 7 6 5 4 3 2 1

For my family,
believers from the beginning.

TO THE READER:

This is a novel. Except for Horace Greeley and James Gordon Bennett, editors, respectively, of the *New York Tribune* and the *New York Herald*, the characters are fictitious.

Still, virtually every incident is based on something that happened.

For the most part, the liberties I have taken have been with time. For instance, the hostilities that form my backdrop actually broke out on Monday, July 13, 1863, ending the following Wednesday. In *Ain't Goin' to Glory* I moved the eruption back ten days: July 3–5.

I did this because I wanted to shine an ironic light on that year's Independence Day, and I apologize to all who view this as liberty degraded to license. It was, at the very least, unscholarly of me.

That having been acknowledged, I think it is also fair to say I have tried hard for real truth. That is, the truth of what it was like to be living in New York City during a certain week of July 1863, when the first draft in the nation's history incited people to riot, rape, pillage, and burn.

DAVID DELMAN

Special thanks to the good people at the Library Company of Philadelphia, who were so endlessly cooperative while I was doing my research.

"Yonder . . .
Balefully glows red Arson—there—and there.
The Town is taken by its rats. . . ."

From *The House-top*, by Herman Melville, July, 1863.

"Ain't goin' for no sojer."

William Jones, Saturday, July 1, 1863. First man ever to be drafted into the United States Army.

Friday June 30, 1863

1

Peter Mackenzie leaned back so that he could more flagrantly wave his built-up boot to attract the waiter's attention. Actually, at that moment, he was as interested in shocking Stephen as he was in anything else, but Stephen was not shocked. It had been many years since Peter had been able to shock him. Or even greatly surprise him.

"Barbarian," Stephen said.

"My glass is empty," Peter said defensively. "Pray, sir, what is a man to do when faced with an empty glass and a raging thirst? Drastic measures, my dear sir. Let the oaf see who he denies—one who has given foot for his country."

Stephen said nothing.

Peter waved his boot again.

Stephen raised up as if to leave, but Peter clutched his arm and said, "Sorry, sorry, sorry." He even managed to look remorseful. As soon as Stephen had reseated himself, however, remorse went west.

"Stephen, you're becoming a stick. I remember a time when you would have relished the approach for its unconventionality."

"When? When I was eight?"

"Were you ever eight? I look at your face and see no trace of the impish lad I fondly recall."

Stephen knew he had never been the impish lad of anyone's recollection and said so, but the words were battered senseless by a sudden barrage of brass band music. It came from the bunting-draped platform not fifteen feet away. The five perpetrators were dressed in gold-trimmed uniforms of union blue—splendid enough to look at but too gaudy to be government issue. They were all red-faced men; red-faced, middle-aged, fat, extravagantly patriotic, and bent on leaving no patron of Delmonico's in doubt as to the imminence of the Fourth of July.

In fact Delmonico's, throughout, was given over to heralding this holiday. Bunting was strewn from the roast-carver's table, raised on a podium of its own as if the roast were the speaker of the house (which, in a sense, it was), to haphazard points helter-skelter across the vast Delmonico's ceiling in a symbolic display of "bombs bursting in air."

In addition there were papier mâché rockets. The railing that separated the band stand from the restaurant floor had become one huge Colonial flag. On each table were red, white, and blue candles. And in each waiter's lapel an artificial boutonniere did its best to convey the true sentiment.

In response to the music, a table of eight officers—all lieutenants—now stood at vibrating attention. Their faces were red, too. They wore their sturdy blue coats over heavy white flannels—and sweated as they sang.

This table was some fifteen feet to the right of the one Stephen Jardine shared with Peter Mackenzie. The band stand was on the left. Thus they were attacked from either side, pincered as it were. Stephen was discovering in himself an even smaller tolerance for patriotic music than he might have predicted. Peter, on the other hand, seemed quite undisturbed. He was intent on getting his glass filled. Having accomplished this, he suddenly grabbed the waiter's belt, preventing him from leaving.

"The bottle, the bottle, man," he said, granting freedom only in

4

exchange for champagne. He reached for Stephen's glass, but Stephen covered it with his hand.

"Have one more with me. Please," Peter said.

"No."

Peter looked at him. "I need you to."

"Oh, for God's sake," Stephen said and removed the obstacle.

Peter filled Stephen's glass. "To us, to friendship. No. To brotherhood, you dear old chap. For he that gets drunk with me tonight shall be my brother, be he ne'er such a stick in the mud."

He raised his glass, waited for Stephen to raise his, then clinked so hard half the contents were sloshed onto Stephen's trousers. Perhaps it was unintentional. Stephen could not be sure.

"How long have we known each other, Stephen?"

"Forever," Stephen said grimly, dabbing at his trousers with a handkerchief.

A man brushed against Peter's chair; a short, plump man twenty years older than the buxom, garishly painted charmer he was leading to the dance floor. The contact he made with the back of the chair was slight enough to have been illusory—on another evening. But clearly Peter was spoiling for something. He was up so quickly he managed to interpose himself between the two, severing them as a couple.

"Clod," he said. "There was a time when Delmonico's was choosier as to its clientele."

Peter's "assailant" looked up at a tall, scowling presence in a major's uniform whose hand hovered disquietingly near a sword hilt. He blanched. A moment ago all had been serene in his pleasure-bound world; now here was this dark-skinned, hawk-nosed savage in uniform, boding him no good.

The woman giggled, too drunk to feel threatened by anything less than a noose and accustomed anyway to bizarre behavior among the males of her acquaintance.

"I . . . I . . ." The plump man's throat trembled. Rheumy eyes swiveled beseechingly in Stephen's direction. That was because Stephen, too, was now on his feet—looking to a desperate man like a possible source of succor.

5

"Have a care, Peter," Stephen said softly.

"A definite provocation," Peter said. "He *looked* at me. Thinks I'm a cripple. Thinks because I'm a cripple he can *look* at me. He cannot."

It was impossible for Stephen to know how seriously Peter meant to be taken. Was he so drunk that he, too, had no idea? Stephen had seen him that way—drunk just above insensibility but showing none of the signs until, at a certain point, he became unconscious.

"What is he talking about?" the fat man asked hoarsely. His glance at Stephen was imploring.

Stephen moved between Peter and his prey, backing Peter off. "Were I you, sir, I would continue on my way," he said. "My friend is—"

"Stay out of this, Stephen. It's none of your affair. I want an apology from him. He has impinged his loutishness on me, and I wish him to confess the crime."

By now of course they had begun to be noticed. The soldiers at the other table broke off their song and, seeing a brother in arms beset—they would view it no other way—began to discuss the possibility of intervention. Stephen sensed a rapidly deteriorating situation. So did the fat man.

"Apologize," Stephen hissed at him.

"I apologize," the fat man said instantly and was shoved by Stephen toward freedom—the blond giggler in tow. Stephen watched after them. He kept himself positioned as an obstacle to pursuit until they reached not merely the dance floor but an exit on the other side of it, through which they vanished. Then he turned to Peter.

"Good night," he said.

Peter, laughing, caught at Stephen's arm again but this time missed.

The night air, while not dry or cool enough to be actually refreshing, was at least an improvement over what had been available inside Delmonico's. Stephen sucked it into his lungs. He looked up. The sky glittered dishearteningly—no sign of rain. And

6

they all badly needed rain, Stephen felt, not just the farmers up beyond 125th Street, but the city folk, too—to cool their tempers. "Hot days, hot heads," his father had been wont to say, packing his medical bag en route to a broken case in point.

He turned toward home, and after a minute or so heard Peter clumping after him.

"I need to talk to you, Stephen," Peter said, the evening's refrain. "Hold up."

Stephen didn't.

A pistol shot. The glass window of a jewelry store directly across the street from him shattered. He looked back. In Peter's hand was the still-smoking revolver. Behind Peter, a hundred yards or so, two police officers were already cautiously on the move, which, Stephen thought, probably meant they were as confused as he was.

Stephen put out his hand. "Give me the pistol," he said.

"Your fault, Stephen. Why wouldn't you wait?"

"Damn you," Stephen said and wrenched the weapon free. He put it in his pocket. By this time the policemen had halved the distance and were close enough now so that Stephen recognized them. They, in turn, recognized him—the larger one naming him to his smaller colleague, sotto voce, the smaller nodding in confirmation. Having thus communicated, they slowed their pace to a sedate amble.

"If you so much as open your mouth," Stephen said to Peter, "I shall hand you over to them."

"And what will they do with me, send me to Devil's Island?"

"I wish," Stephen said. "Evening, Sergeants."

"Evening, Mr. Jardine," the smaller one said. His glance was fixed on the dramatically shattered window, but he said nothing to indicate that he took its condition amiss.

"Sergeant O'Neill [smaller], Sergeant Prendergast [larger], I believe you know Dr. Mackenzie . . . Major Mackenzie, these days."

They nodded.

Peter grinned and swayed just a little, just enough, however, to

7

attract the attention of professionals. Flickers of edification passed over each sergeant's face.

Prendergast spoke to his colleague while jerking his chin toward the jewelry store and its interesting window. "That will be attracting attention soon enough. Had I best find a precinct runner to tell them there we have it in hand?"

O'Neill nodded, and Prendergast began retracing his steps. They all watched him. When he reached the corner, they saw him put his police whistle to his lips. The sound was piercing.

Peter positioned his hands for cuffing. "At your disposal, Sergeant."

Stephen slapped Peter's hands away. "There is an explanation for all this, Sergeant," he said.

"Yes, sir."

"Will it offend you if I give it to Chief Inspector Brautigan?"

For the first time O'Neill smiled. A small smile, but a significant one. It placed the event in that catchall labeled, for the sake of convenience, "family matters."

"No need to put yourself out, sir. I'll be glad to do that for you."

"Thank you, Sergeant."

"Then good night to you, sir."

Seeing that Peter was about to speak, Stephen pulled him away roughly and kept him moving as quickly as his special boot would permit.

He turned back once to see O'Neill looking after him. O'Neill saluted, a gesture of sympathy—a drunk was a drunk, O'Neill seemed to be saying, and a trouble to all his friends. Or at least Stephen construed the gesture to mean that, because it was certainly what *he* was feeling. He found a hack, shoved Peter into it, and climbed in after him. To the driver he named the Metropolitan Hospital where Peter had a temporary billet.

"No, no," Peter said. "Must celebrate my escape from Devil's Island. Must drink to you, Stephen. Sturdy, ever-dependable Stephen without whom . . . *And* to the celebrated Chief Inspector John Brautigan without whom . . ."

He fell asleep.

8

Stephen studied him. In repose the lines of dissatisfaction around his forty-three-year-old mouth had smoothed, and Stephen felt an unexpected pang. This angered him. He was not eager to feel sympathy for Peter. As a deterrent, he reminded himself that not all friendships lasted forever. A friendship could be like a once favorite suit. It could be outgrown. It could wear out and have to be replaced. He thought of other, better friends—John Brautigan, for instance.

The horse clip-clopped its message to the night.

Suddenly, Stephen, too, fell asleep. In sleep, ironically, his head drifted onto Peter's shoulder.

9

2

With the departure of his sergeants, Chief Inspector Brautigan felt the silence of the house in a way that had become all too familiar to him. It was an affronting silence; a silence that, in persisting, seemed to mount indictments against him. He had hoped to keep the sergeants with him as a buffer, but to no avail. They had slipped out on him. O'Neill and Prendergast—old shoes at the precinct—had never been comfortable with him in his house. They both remembered Nora Brautigan too well for that.

And yet on one level Nora's behavior to them had always been faultless. The correct smile, the correct query as to the well-being of their families, the correct offer of cold drinks on hot days and hot drinks on . . . faultless. Even gracious. But neither of the sergeants were fools, and both had readily perceived—and accepted as substantive—the tacit though constant underlying message. Which was that the descendant of native-born school teachers—on both sides—was a personage not to be compared to the descendants of County Clare tinkers once removed. And that, as a corollary, it was to be understood that sergeants and chief inspectors had only the color of their uniforms in common.

Dead three years, Nora was still powerful enough in 124 Bleecker to discomfit sergeants even as redoubtable as these. Steely-eyed everywhere else, they became shifty-eyed here, as if searching corners for ghostly emanations.

The incident of the shattered window was briskly reported. Not three minutes later, the door had shut behind them.

So Brautigan poured himself a lonely whisky. He thought first about Stephen and Peter Mackenzie, and, as always, was irritated by how exploitative that relationship was. The man was a powder keg looking for a place to explode. Why couldn't Stephen see that? But of course Stephen did. Knowing this to be the case, Brautigan made his customary stretch for a more temperate view. There were entries on both sides of the Jardine-Mackenzie ledger. Fairness insisted on that acknowledgement, and Stephen had often given him chapter and verse about how valiant Boy Mackenzie had been in behalf of Boy Jardine. It's just that he, Brautigan, had never cottoned to Mackenzie, never trusted him. Too bloody handsome, for one thing. When they were like that, they were too bloody in love with themselves.

He thought this with a vehemence that initially surprised him. A moment later he had his explanation. The insight made him wince. As with Mackenzie, so it was with Michael, his son. He recalled now what Stephen had said to him, appositely, a year ago, after the first time Michael had abandoned home and hearth.

"We're all self-lovers, John, but Michael's more so. He's never out of his own thoughts. When Nora was alive, they wrote the book of Michael together, a day-by-day collaboration. So that now he no longer has any detachment about himself. He's the protagonist, the rest of us merely gauzy minor characters. Even you."

Brautigan had resisted it then. Stephen being dour, he told himself. He accepted it now, all right, but God almighty, what was to be done about it?

The sound on the back porch turned out to be a stray cat. For a moment he had thought it might be Michael having forgotten his latchkey. He knew very well of course that Michael didn't have a latchkey anymore. That hadn't stopped him. Just showed the

11

willful way a man's mind could work. Causing a man a bit of extra pain, who didn't need any extras along that line.

The quarrel had begun mildly enough, not much different than any of their other quarrels on the same subject. As he sat down for breakfast, Michael had informed him that he'd go directly from his job at Brooks Brothers Clothing Emporium to the firehouse. It was volunteer recruitment night, he'd said, and he'd be late getting home. And then he'd added that gratuitous slam at George Tolliver.

"If we had someone other than a fuddy-duddy for a chief, recruitment meets might go easier."

Brautigan had tried to ignore it, tried to pretend he was as eager for his bacon and eggs as he had been the moment before. And it was not of course that he himself was so high on George Tolliver, who fit Michael's description snugly if the truth be known. It was just that both knew to whom Tolliver was being invidiously compared.

"He's honest," Brautigan had said finally. "Make a ten dollar contribution to George Tolliver's company, and you'll see it go for equipment."

"Who cares?"

Brautigan looked at him. "Honesty don't matter in your book, Michael?"

The boy got up from the table, shoving his plate away. "I'm leaving. I'm late."

"Stay a minute."

"I can't. I'm—"

"Sit!"

Michael sat—not cowed, but not quite nerved yet to open rebellion. A hair's breadth short of it, Brautigan thought, with the kind of dismay that stems from being wrong in every possible way, including tactically. But he persisted nonetheless, though he did manage to soften his tone.

"Michael, son, all I meant—"

"I know what you meant. Haven't I heard it a dozen times already? You meant that George Tolliver is as straight as a

12

flagpole. But Mr. Tolliver's fire company is the joke of the city, just the same. That's *why* we have so many recruitment meetings, and why they last so long. Because nobody wants to join a fire company that never gets where it's going until thirty minutes after everybody else does. And which can't shoot water more than a dozen feet because all its hoses have holes. And which last month lost two horses dead of old age. While Boss Tyrell's Tiger Heads . . . ah, what's the use."

"Boss Tyrell's a crook."

"Pa, I don't want to hear that any more. I'm tired of it. Everybody knows—" He broke off suddenly. And suspiciously.

"Everybody knows what?"

"That you and Mr. Tyrell don't like each other." But it was so lame and makeshift a conclusion that it was easy for Brautigan to guess what it was replacing.

"Everybody knows I'm jealous of him? Is that what everybody knows?"

Michael maintained a glum silence.

"Is that what *you* know, Michael?"

"What I know is it's none of my business," Michael said sourly.

Brautigan took a deep breath. "Sounds to me like some of the boss's Tammany boys have been at you. That the case?"

Michael shrugged.

"Is it?"

"Been at me? What does that mean? I have friends in Tammany Hall. Sure I do. Everybody who wants to get ahead in this city has friends in Tammany. There isn't any other way."

"Isn't there?"

Michael exploded. "Je-sus! Am I to hear again about how wonderful life is when you get to be a chief inspector?"

"I never—"

"That is not what I call getting ahead. I want more. I want a big house and a slap-up carriage and slap-up clothes, and you can't get that on a salary. Pa, listen to me. For once in your life truly listen. We're not all the same."

"What you mean is you and I are not the same."

13

"Yes. That's what I mean. One of these days you'll marry Rosie Shannon, move her in here . . . or a house just like it . . . and you'll be happy. More power to you. I'd be suffocated. I'm not saying you're wrong and I'm right. I'm saying I want to go my own way, that's all."

"Quite a speech, Michael."

"You've heard it before."

"Your own way. Crooked or not?"

"Oh, for God's sake."

"And get the big money however you can? Answer me, Michael."

"I have answered you. Dozens and dozens of times. Why aren't you as tired of this conversation as I am?"

Brautigan forced himself into silence. He made himself get up and go to the window. He forced himself to stand there looking out until he felt sure of his temper. And only then did he turn and speak.

"No way to have us both, Michael. Terence Tyrell and me go off in opposite directions."

Michael kept silent.

"You understand what I'm saying? It's not possible for you to walk those two sides of the street, Tyrell's and mine. It can't be done."

"You want me out of here?"

"You know better than that."

Michael rose. His fists, almost as large as his father's, were clenching and unclenching, and he studied them bemusedly, as if he had not put them to the work in which they were engaged. But in a moment they were hidden in his pockets, and what he had not been ready for earlier he was ready for now, Brautigan knew helplessly.

"Well, maybe it's a pretty good idea anyway," Michael said, eyes hard.

And when Brautigan returned that night the premises had been vacated.

Still, the strange thing is how relieved he had been at first. He

14

had felt released. An explosion. A catharsis. Nothing hidden and festering anymore. Better for both of them. If they could not live together under the same roof, so be it. Best acknowledge it. Come to terms with it. You could be father to a son and not see him every day—of course you could.

Even the quiet of the house had failed to trouble him at first. In fact he had reveled in it. Neatness and orderliness were restored, states Michael warred against. The house pleased him.

By the second month, however, a change had set in. No contact with Michael, no messages of any kind. Only the occasional report from Rosie Shannon to indicate that Michael still walked the same earth he did. It preyed on him. He told himself it was exactly what he had expected, that it was foolish to be upset by something so predictable, but the house began to seem less comfortable. Comfort had been only a veneer. Flake after flake of it peeled, and loneliness was beneath.

He had gone over the quarrel endlessly. How could he *not* have warned Michael against Tyrell? How could a father see his son threatened by that kind of corruption and not do what he could to save him from it?

By now, the third month of Michael's absence, loneliness, anger and regret had combined in a rich mixture. It seeped into brain crevices. It impaired the capacity for thinking clearly about anything else. And there *were* things to think about.

There was Rosie to think about. "You'll marry Rosie Shannon," Michael had said in that cocksure way of his—the protagonist arranging a plot development for a couple of gauzy minor characters.

What, to Michael, were the twenty years that separated the two people he had so breezily bracketed? Not enough to slow him down. Well they gave his father pause, all right.

He moved to the mirror over the mantel, seeking the reassurance there he could find on certain days. Not there today. He had known it wouldn't be. Oh, the bone structure was still reasonably pure, the hair remarkably free of gray at forty-five. Yes, but now

15

look in the eyes. It was there the telltale signs lay. The tiredness was in the eyes; the gray in the soul.

Sinking back into his chair, he stuck his legs out into the room as far as they would go. He heard the cat again. Not for an instant now did he think it might be Michael. He retrieved his glass, sloshed the whisky in it, then took a deep pull. A moment later he flung the bottle, still three-quarters full, into the fireplace. It was either that or finish it.

3

Rosie got Stephen Jardine III to bed easily enough for a change. Only two extra stories, only one extra glass of water, half a dozen extra kisses.

For once she would not have to rush like a madcap to be ready when John Brautigan came by. Not that John ever complained. He was an angel about that as he was about most things . . . everything . . . except the thing that mattered most. Stop that, she warned herself, you promised to be good. Being good meant compliance with a certain inward standard she had structured for herself in the form of a vow—that the next time the subject . . . *the* subject . . . arose between them it would be John who brought it up.

John—what if they had never found each other? That was a possibility so close to being a probability that sometimes just thinking about it made her break out in patches of unladylike perspiration on afternoons far less sweltering than this one. They had always known each other of course; "good-dayed" each other for years without forming anything that could be described as a connection. Actually, Michael had been the inadvertent fishing line. And how funny all that had been, from beginning to end.

Governor Blanchard's party to celebrate John's ascendancy to the chief inspectorship. Michael dancing with her twice, the second time pivotal. Fifteen, Michael had been then, and full of brass. Imagine—asking her *twice*, and she six years his senior. And not taking no for an answer either. No stammering shyness from our Michael when it came to girls. Why should there be? He did nothing but succeed with them. Nora Brautigan's blue eyes and blond curls and his own glib tongue there to account for it. She remembered teasing him about his self-assurance. Even more vividly—things being as they were with our Michael today—she remembered his response.

"Girls are easy. That's because they don't matter. Men matter. They have everything."

What had he meant by everything? He hadn't been willing to say. Only a fifteen-year-old after all, he hadn't been eager to articulate what he thought about power as a shaper of lives. But he knew how it worked, Rosie thought.

Because he'd seen the effects of it close to home. Without the Blanchard scholarship, even so exceptional a person as his own father might have stayed stuck on Chrystie Street. Rosie understood about that. During one of the several low-ebb periods in the Shannon family fortune she had known the jealous strength of the street's downward pull—Tyrells, Royces, Murphys, and all that unlovely breed piling their weight on, green with envy the lot of them.

It was midway through the second polka that Michael tried to kiss her. He had whirled her into a dark corner formed by the intersecting eaves of a Blanchard gable. Amused by him, she might have permitted the kiss. It was the cockiness that had to be punished. No one—particularly an urchin—had the right to be that confident about Rosie Shannon.

As he leaned forward, she stepped out of the way. Seeing that he had slightly unbalanced himself, she pulled hard on his collar, causing a dramatic thud as head met cherry wood paneling. From

18

across the ballroom, John had witnessed the whole absurd little comedy without being in the least amused. He came steaming toward them, face pale and angry. Her honor, she knew, was about to be defended. Before he could speak, however, she had inserted herself neatly into his embrace and danced him halfway back across the room again.

"Not a word," she had said, "Or I promise to dissolve in tears. And how will you explain that to Governor Blanchard?"

She heard him growl something but then relax. By this time Michael was Michael again. Give him his due—the grin and tug of the forelock accompanying had been good-natured. A few minutes later, he left the party. Or so he subsequently told her. She hadn't noticed. Accidentally her cheek had made contact with the broadcloth of John's shirt. With that unprepossessing little touch, he became part of the texture of her life. Why should such a cause have such an effect? In explanation, if put to it, she could have furnished a list of John Brautigan particulars—ticking off qualities such as gentleness, kindness, rock-ribbed dependability. But the fact was she hadn't asked herself why. And did so only idly now. *Why* wasn't a Rosie Shannon kind of question. *When?* Now that was a Rosie Shannon question, for certain sure, and she had asked it often enough, one way or another, to heat her cheeks whenever she recalled her efforts. But not again. Her vow stood firm against it.

As devilment would have it, however, it was not John but Margaret Jardine who brought the matter up, and—to Rosie's annoyance—not seriously either. Offhandedly almost. As no more than a conversation opener, Rosie could tell, from the ardent way Margaret was picking at a lace under-bodice thread. She was preoccupied. With what? With the unexpected return (from the Army of the Potomac) of Peter Mackenzie. And if that were granted, did it signify more than just hot-weather nerves? Rosie wasn't sure.

Margaret had found Rosie stretched on her bed, luxuriating in the bonus minutes young Stephen had unexpectedly supplied. Unceremoniously, she had fired off her question.

19

Instead of answering, Rosie got off the bed and shut the door her cousin had left gaping. "Must the whole world be a party to my business?"

"What makes you think the whole world cares a—" But then she caught herself. "Forgive me, Rosie. My brains are frying. If it doesn't rain soon I shall trade New York City for someplace more congenial—the Sahara, for instance."

Rosie decided then it was not the weather that was most responsible for Margaret's twitching. Out of sympathy with her at the moment, however, Rosie was inclined to let her stew. In the next moment she thought she saw real trouble on Margaret's face and let her irritation shrink to allow for more cousinly feelings.

They *were* cousinly now—close, confidential, mutually appreciative—but it had not always been the case. As children they had watched each other from opposite sides of a social and financial gulf. It had seemed unbridgeable. Margaret's antecedents were rich and prominent. Warp and woof, the Blanchards were woven into the fabric of New York's history: Margaret's father had succeeded her grandfather as the state's governor. Rosie's family, a collateral Blanchard branch, had far less to be said for it. And, over the years, much to be said against it, in inner family circles. For one thing, in a variety of ill-conceived, ill-timed, and ill-managed ventures, it had contrived to lose most of its money. Respectability followed fortune then, when two generations back these wayward Blanchards had traded the dignity of Episcopalianism for the raffishness, to say the least, of Roman Catholicism. Among their sterner critics, the lapse had been regarded as unforgivable, the rupture permanent. As Margaret's grandmother had bruisingly put it: "On Gramercy Place, we don't *know* Catholics." And *Rosie's* grandmother had found herself cut.

But the moderates—among them Margaret's parents—had not been routed. Patiently, they made the case for tolerance and eventually had their way. Not quite a reconciliation at first but at least an amelioration: Rosie's mother and Margaret's began to nod to each other on the Fifth Avenue. *Large* family occasions—

20

Margaret's introduction to society, for instance—had included Rosie and Mrs. Shannon, by then, conveniently, a widow.

Margaret and Rosie, however, had remained wary of each other. Inevitably, Rosie thought Margaret the very definition of a snob. Margaret's appraisal was equally slighting. She regarded Rosie as the quintessential country cousin—a hoyden, a tomboy—who refused to be guided by someone older (three years) and infinitely more experienced. ("I declare, Rosie Shannon, you couldn't be more Blanchardy stiff-necked if you were a *real* Blanchard.")

But then came the sudden, shocking rupture of Margaret's engagement to Peter Mackenzie—and on the heels of that, her two year exodus to Paris.

On her return, Margaret had seemed to Rosie so changed as to have been reborn. Through the Jardines, they met more frequently—Dr. Jardine (Stephen's father) was physician to both families. Soon Margaret's marriage to Stephen brought the cousins even closer, a circumstance that, in effect, opened their eyes to each other. Beneath the obvious superficial differences they discovered an affinity of outlook that could make them friends. Two events served as bonding. The first was the death of Rosie's mother. The Jardines took Rosie into their house. Margaret's support was not only staunch but remarkably sensitive, and Rosie would never forget that. Even when Margaret was at her most Blanchardy, Rosie could temper her response by recalling the softness of voice and hand, without which, in trauma's early aftermath, sleep would have been impossible.

The other event was the birth of baby Stephen. Rosie fell violently in love. She appointed herself unofficial nanny and was, in turn, named official godmother. Margaret, dutiful though scarcely doting, had said, "Heaven knows what you see in him, Rosie. He's a sweet boy, of course he is, but I will not *begin* to take him seriously until he has some teeth and ideas in his head."

Now fanning herself savagely (and counterproductively) it was clear she took the late June heat as a personal affront—Margaret joined Rosie on the bed, wriggling to achieve a disproportionate

21

share of the available space. Rosie let her. It was too hot for undue concern about the principles of things.

"Really, I expected you to have settled John Brautigan's hash by now," Margaret said.

Rosie's reply was to the effect that whether she had or hadn't was her business, not Margaret's, and at any rate John Brautigan was not a man who jumped at the crack of a female whip. "If he was I wouldn't want him. And besides *he* isn't what you have on your mind anyway."

Margaret looked at her, got up from the bed, and went to the window. "There goes prissy Sue Ann Northrop and her ironclad mother steaming across Gramercy Park. Hell bent for bible class, no doubt."

Rosie smothered a laugh. "Margaret, you're too free with that kind of remark."

Margaret turned, the better to glare at her. "Hoity-toity Mrs. Northrop. Mean-spirited women, the both of them. All the Northrops. They want to keep everyone out of heaven who isn't Northropian."

"All the same she can—"

"Can what? Cut me dead? Delete me from her next cotillion? Nonsense. She wouldn't dare. Haven't I told you again and again, my child? If one has a stout heart and good family connections, one can do pretty much as one pleases in this city."

"Hoity-toity Margaret Blanchard," Rosie said.

Margaret's eyes sparked, but the anger melted almost as it got underway. She then made two or three quick passes with her Chinese fan and abandoned that, too, as inefficacious in its own right. "I don't know why I bother with these things. They never do any good, do they? Do you want it? It's new."

"I have a new one."

"Did you ever see such a cruelly hot day?"

"Yes. About this time last year."

"Stop that. I won't be teased when I'm feeling so utterly . . ."

"Frazzled. But why are you?"

22

"I just this minute got finished explaining. Rosie Shannon, you have a way of not listening that is downright aboriginal."

"Whatever that means," Rosie said and shut her eyes. She tried to be as still as possible, but even so she felt moisture begin to gather under her arms and in the hollow of her neck. She'd get John to drive her out to the new park today. It was lovely there. Fountains and other cool places. Places for them to be alone. Places in which—

She heard Margaret say, "Young Stephen went off all right, did he? Didn't stage his usual holy war against sleep?"

"He was a pet."

"You're a much better mother than I am. That's because you're far less selfish. It's natural for you to love. Whereas I have to work at it—except when it comes to loving myself, of course. What I'd make is a good general. A few like me, and perhaps old Abe could end this war."

"A woman general. I think I'd like to see that."

"You will one day."

"Anyway, there's nothing wrong with you as a mother. You're a slow starter, that's all. You'll be first rate when Stephen gets older. You're that kind."

Margaret smiled. "Thank you, dear Rosie." After a moment she added, "I *am* feeling frazzled."

"But not from the heat."

"No."

"What is it, Margaret?"

"Nothing. Foolishness."

"The same old foolishness?"

But that was too close to the bone. Blanchardy to beat the band, eyes slitted, arms folded across her chest, Margaret said, "Don't be a bloody fool."

She went out, slamming the door.

Rosie shut her eyes again. She heard the door open, but her eyes remained shut.

Margaret kissed Rosie's hair. "Damn and blast," she said softly and went out again.

23

From Stephen Jardine's diary. Friday, June 30:

. . . he has my nose, a noticeable nose. Well, it's the Jardine nose and no mistake. And no help for it, so he must content himself, young Stephen.

And he *does* have her eyes, there's compensation. Dark blue; anger turns them even darker. In sum, I find him a satisfactory piece of work and predict he will surpass his father on all counts. His mother says she wishes him only a better temper. Well, it's the Jardine temper, and no mistake about that either. Bending to him, I fixed his coverlet, kissed him, and wondered how much longer I would be permitted to do that. My own father, fond as he was, stopped, I think, when I was six. Custom doth make cowards of us all.

After which I took root at my study window—one trouser leg on, one off—admiring the stars. Many stars. I sought poetic images. I decided the sky was . . . vast. And that I was . . . small. And something else, but I forget now what it was.

After which—the labor of the pantaloons completed—I found myself in my shirt uncertain what to do next. I made for the couch and stretched upon it. I heard sounds. Lifted head, forced lids open, discovered Margaret. Like a ghost, she stood at the threshhold in her filmy white nightdress watching me somberly. "How drunk?" she asked.

"Very."

She came forward, slipped onto the couch next to me and held my head against her breast. "You should be ashamed."

"He is an old friend. He told me I was badly needed."

"I don't want to hear about it. Nor him, for that matter."

"Margaret—"

"Hush," she said.

I must have dozed. I have no idea for how long, but when I woke Margaret was gone. Knowing I would sleep no more tonight, I struggled to my desk and the solace of this journal. But the better

24

part of a quarter hour passed during which I stared at it unproductively. It was as if suddenly, while my attention was diverted, a glass pane had been slipped between pen and page. Or between the conceptual and operational compartments of my brain. It was . . . it is . . . as if nothing I want to say is safe to say; as if once said it becomes imperishable.

Saturday July 1, 1863

Knives of sunshine sliced in from both sides of the Third Avenue omnibus, yet Stephen Jardine shivered. He felt ravaged. Which is to say he felt precisely as a man should who, the night before, had spent more hours than he had bargained for at Delmonico's—gorging on oysters, swilling champagne.

Dismally, he glanced about at his heat-stupified fellow passengers: laborers in sweat-soaked shirtsleeves; pink-faced butcher boys in coats once white, now polka-dotted with blood and other stains; fat young women with runny-nosed babies; one black-whiskered *bon vivant* with collar miraculously crisp, but from whom the scent of ten thousand cigars was inextricable; and a bald and bullet-headed former infantry sergeant—the ectoplast of stripes still on his sleeve—with a stare so vacant one could construe him as blind though he was not. A crew, Stephen thought, unqualified to be balm for the wound in his state of health.

Peter Mackenzie had a wound, too—his somewhat more dramatic. Gone was his left foot. Sheared off at the ankle at Shiloh. He professed not to be bothered by the loss.

"Merely a temporary inconvenience," he had said last night.

"Temporary?"

"In a sense. In the sense that I have absolutely no intention of coming out of this war alive. And besides, what need has a surgeon for feet? I mean, sir, as long as he has his strong right arm he can be propped up while he hacks away with the best of them."

The omnibus skidded to a skull-shattering stop near the withered carcass of a horse, which had died heaven knew when and would be hauled off by the city's scandalous sanitation force surely before the close of the decade. In the meantime, it contributed its share to the general aura of pestilence and putrefaction. July was ever thus. One could smell cholera around the corner.

Tenth Street, usually a one-passenger-on, one-off hiatus, was not so today. Today the conductor did an endless business while Stephen flirted with the notion of transferring to a hack. A brief flirtation. For even if he found one, it would have to cope with the same nightmarish array of carriages, wagon carts, stages, and scarlet-and-yellow omnibuses that his own scarlet-and-yellow omnibus was at war with. A crisscrossing, zigzagging, unremitting flow of traffic, the evils of which were compounded by the occasional sporty trotter darting toward a highly illusory opening and locking wheels, often as not, with a sturdier vehicle to the detriment of all.

Stephen clenched his teeth and made a heroic effort to shut out the din. How much of what Peter had said was worth sober concern? How much was it the man talking and how much the champagne? How did one go about answering questions like that when the subject was as in love with enigma as Peter Mackenzie had been all his life?

The precise term of their friendship was thirty-five years. Fond fathers—doctors and close associates as well as close friends— had introduced their sons, hoping for the best. At first it had seemed as if they would be disappointed. The boys had not liked each other. Natural rivals, they demonstrated this on every field available to them—in their schools, on their streets . . . Peter, never shy, had been the more socially adroit. And the better

30

scholar. Stephen, though a shade smaller and slighter, had blood-ied Peter's nose often enough during these years to have been finally—though tacitly—acknowledged the tougher battler. But when Stephen was twelve, scarlet fever had almost killed him. He survived it, an emaciated version of the boy he had been. That—in the paradoxical way trouble has of being therapeutic—had ended the animosity. Delicate and vulnerable during his recuperation, Stephen, somewhat to his surprise, found himself enjoying the protection of a strong and resourceful older brother.

Two years later Peter's parents had been lost at sea on their way back from England. He had come to live with the Jardines. In a way, then, a role reversal had taken place. Stunned by what had happened to him, unable to understand it in terms of anything he had been taught about a beneficent deity, Peter had crawled into silence. It was as if he had found a cave deep within himself and had burrowed into it for safety. Months of this. A sallow-faced, sullen boy haunted the Jardine brownstone. Answers in monosyl-lables when they came at all; meals in his room and only when famished; the upper story of the house his self-imposed prison. But with Dr. Jardine prescribing, Stephen had administered steady doses of patience and affection. This had worn down and eventually vanquished the disease. Or if not actually vanquished, had at least driven it into remission, the flare-ups occasional and manageable.

"Are you in any kind of trouble?" Stephen had asked at one point during the previous night's garish activities.

"Serious trouble."

After considering this for a moment, Stephen said, "I think we are talking at cross-purposes."

"Do you mean has someone caught me cheating at whist or women?"

"I suppose the latter is what I had in mind."

"I am in serious trouble only with myself. The fact is I bore me. To death," he added, while engaging in that offensive rigmarole with his special shoe, an act of deliberate self-mockery.

Stephen tried to imagine the state of suicidal boredom. He

could not. At forty-one he found life consistently interesting. Even when it punished him. Even when it filled him with despair. And yet there was Peter, weary of his life to the point where he sought opportunities to throw it away. If the reports of his behavior at Shiloh were not exaggerated, they certainly underscored an instance. Down with the scalpel, up with the sword. And, mounted on a stray horse, off he had gone, charging into a battery of Gatling guns, scattering Johnny Rebs. It was a piece of madness that, by rights, should have won him his goal. That is, the mention he earned in dispatches should have been posthumous.

Not that he had missed the mark by all that much. Mission accomplished, the horse had celebrated by stepping on a land mine. As a result Peter was just now coming to the end of five months spent in one hospital or another, the early part of which had been a time of nip and tuck—at issue not only his foot but his life.

The horsecar lurched, causing the sportsman to spangle Stephen with cigar ash. They glared at each other a moment or so before yielding to heat and sinking back to apathy.

Sixteenth Street. The provost marshal's office was at Forty-sixth, and, at the pace of these Percherons, an eternity away. Well, forty-five minutes anyway. Would there be trouble today? Greeley insisted there would not be. Horace Greeley, with his child's face and his long white hair, milking his mutton-chop whiskers and stroking his paunch, while he claimed an insight into the heart of the working-class New Yorker that was matched by no man else.

"Your working-class New Yorker is a patriot, sir," he was wont to say, digging into the hoard of apples (brain food, he insisted) that filled his desk drawer daily. "Above all else a patriot. I promise you, sir, he will always place the interests of his country first."

Patriot he undoubtedly had been in April of '61 when the rebels fired on Fort Sumter. Who could easily forget the flags, the horns, the drums, the endless parades. Nightly, Broadway had been a sea of warlike bodies, marching in candlelight procession. How caught up in it all Stephen himself had been. How furious with

32

the South for its disunionizing arrogance. How eager to strike his personal blow. Never mind that he was overage. Lincoln had called; Jardine was on fire to respond.

"You will find soldiering intolerable," Greeley had said. "Oh, you're brave enough to be sure, but you know how much you hate taking orders, even those as sensible as mine."

But between April of '61 and July of '63 had come Bull Run (twice), Shiloh, Chancellorsville, Fredericksburg, and so on, a series of disillusionments. And by now, it was obvious to Stephen, your New York working man's stock of patriotism had been drastically depleted. The parades were infrequent these days.

The muttering against the Negro was more open, particularly down on the wharves where white and black stevedores lined up daily for the same limited number of jobs. But it did not follow that what was obvious to Stephen Jardine was obvious to Horace Greeley. The latter saw only what he wished to see. It was a capability he had in common with all great men, Stephen thought wryly.

The horses lumbered to a stop at Twenty-first Street. Had Stephen been homeward bound, Gramercy Place was but a block to the north. The pounding in his head made him yearn for it. An instant later the thought was gone, as forgotten as if it had never existed, and Stephen Jardine, managing editor of the New York *Tribune*, instinctively, though unconsciously, edged forward on his seat.

Two of the five people who boarded the omnibus at Twenty-first Street were very much worth a journalist's notice, the woman because of who she was, the man because of what.

The woman, soberly dressed in black bombazine, heavily veiled, was about thirty-five. She was known to Stephen—Mary Haines, once the owner of a Mercer Street brothel famous for its opulence and sophistication. She had lost it in a poker game, famous in its own right.

She paid her sixpence and glided farther into the car. Graceful, unhurried. Hers was the kind of veteran coolness developed in the

33

opera/theater/academy wars: fifty lorgnettes instantly fired at her whenever she entered a parquet circle. She nodded at Stephen. He nodded in return. Though the seat next to him was vacant, she chose to bypass it. In the back row she sat alone, pretending uninterest in the excitement she had caused. Experienced observers of Mary Haines (Stephen, for instance) knew differently, of course. Her lips formed the foretaste of a smile. Against her honey-colored cheek, her fan was only seemingly languid. Not for a minute did Stephen doubt her destination: the provost marshal's. He was sure of this because New York had been buzzing for weeks about the first military draft in the nation's history, and Mary was certain to encounter some old friends there, whose twinges of discomfort she was certain to enjoy. Just as she was enjoying Stephen's now.

The man who had followed Mary aboard was not obviously in her company, and yet it was Stephen's sudden conviction that he, too, was bound for the provost marshal's. He was tall and well-made. Early thirties. He was a soldier and wore the blue jacket and red Zouave trousers of the famous Fifty-fourth Massachusetts. He was a lieutenant, and . . . he was black.

All New York knew that Negro regiments existed. They had been organized first as support troops, with weapons kept from them. Then, with the Emancipation on New Year's Day, restrictions had finally been lifted and black troops sent into action. To the surprise of many and chagrin of some, they had done well. What was less known to New Yorkers, however, is that among these black regiments was a sprinkling of black officers. On Omnibus "Front to Bleecker," he caused a stir.

"Not next to me, nigger."

It was the former sergeant, no longer vacant-eyed. He was alert now, body stiffly held. The black man did not break stride. He went by, in fact, as if nothing had been said. Stephen made room and beckoned.

"Thank you, sir," the black officer said, accepting the invitation.

There was no South in his voice. It was clear, educated. Educated Negroes, while not unique in Stephen's acquaintance, were rare enough to remain a somewhat heady experience. Realizing that he was staring, he shook himself out of it. He extended his hand.

"My name is Jardine. I work for Horace Greeley's *Tribune*."

"Richard Frazier, sir."

"You know our newspaper?"

"Oh yes. Mr. Greeley has always been kind to us."

To the assemblage at large, still without turning, the ex-sergeant said, "In Washington we don't let niggers ride our horsecars. Sambo stays out in the mud where he belongs."

"I can do something about that," Stephen said.

Frazier shook his head. "It doesn't matter. Tell me, sir, why has there been so little news of the draft in the *Tribune*?"

"Not just the *Tribune*."

"That is correct. Not just the *Tribune*. In the *Herald* this morning I had to turn to the back page before I found an account."

"I think perhaps we are afraid of it. And drawn to it, too." Stephen paused. "May I inquire, sir, if you yourself are on your way to the provost marshal's?"

"I am."

"To see which black men are drafted?"

His smile was cool. "I think you know as well as I there will be no black men drafted today. New York City is not eager to put a gun in a black man's hand. No, sir, I go to the provost marshal's for the same reason you do. Drawn to it, sir."

Stephen studied him. Then after a moment, he nodded. "I see," he said. "At least I think I do."

Frazier was about to speak when once again he was preempted: "Worse than niggers is nigger-lovers."

Stephen, face heated, was on his feet. Seeing him coming, the bald-headed man got to his feet, too—hand snaking purposefully toward an inner pocket. It never arrived. Stephen whacked its knuckles with his cane, eliciting a high-pitched and distinctly gratifying yowl.

"Driver," he called out over this, "you have a passenger wishing to debark."

35

"Like hell—"

"*Now,*" Stephen said and swung the cane again in a trajectory that started at the man's eyes, then skinned his nose, before coming to a shattering end, literally, on the steel backrest of his seat. The cane was now half its original length but made up in menace what it lacked in size. Its end was jagged and lethal-looking. With this, Stephen, like an impatient shepherd, herded the man down the aisle.

The omnibus conductor proved cooperative. Cheers from the passengers greeted his action. Obviously, the ex-soldier was not the type to form natural alliances.

"Bastard. Toff son of a bitch. Worse than nigger-lovers is toffs. You'll get yours. John J. Evarts makes you a promise."

By this time, however, John J. Evarts was marooned on Broadway, brandishing a helpless fist as the omnibus put distance between him and it.

Stephen enjoyed the man's frustration. In fact, he was feeling rather pleased about the whole encounter until he turned and saw this was not a view shared by Lieutenant Frazier.

"Thank you, sir. Much obliged," Frazier said in a tone that made it sufficiently clear he was not. "And good day."

"Good day?" A quick glance had informed Stephen they were still some dozen and a half blocks short of the provost marshal's office.

Frazier smiled distantly. A moment later, without waiting for it to achieve a full stop, he leaped from the omnibus.

Stephen heard Mary calling his name and went to join her.

"Apparently I acted foolishly," he said. "I wonder how."

"If you were black you'd know. A black man has his own way of dealing with scum like that. And he doesn't need the buckra to help him."

"By buckra I take it you mean folk like me."

"Folk of the white persuasion, yes."

"He *resented* me helping him?"

"Yes, but that's not the point. The point is he didn't *need* you

36

helping him. And he certainly didn't need all those people feeling so patronizingly sorry for him."

"He might have taken a moment to explain that," Stephen said.

She shrugged. "In the first place, it would have have taken more than a moment. And in the second place, I have the feeling about Lieutenant Frazier that he's not a man who relishes the act of explaining. Anyway, I'm furious with you. One of these days that hot head of yours is going to get you killed, and then what will I do? I mean any idiot would have recognized the type who hides guns and things in his sleeves and boots. Any idiot except you, of course."

"You know him? Lieutenant Frazier, I mean."

"I met him today for the first time. He came bearing a letter of introduction." Malicious pause. "From his father."

"His father?"

She kept silent.

Something clicked. "Frazier," he said. "Might he be the son of the Reverend Clement Frazier?"

"He might be."

Stephen cleared his throat, but then did not speak after all.

She laughed the laugh she was famous for. Even in that stultifying omnibus, expressions lightened in response. And darkened the next instant as their owners realized what they were about. "A courtesy call, my pet, and no more. I knew Reverend Frazier when I was a child," she said.

"When you were a child in Boston?"

"I was never a child in Boston."

"It is my recollection you have been a child in Boston, Philadelphia, Chicago, Kansas City, Richmond, and Toronto. At least so you have said to me at different times."

"Nonsense. I was a child in Syracuse, New York. It was there I met Reverend Frazier, though he was not Reverend Frazier then. Then he was naught but a runaway darky named Clem."

"Taken in by your banker father, who—before he fell on the evil days you have so often recounted to me in detail—fed, clothed and educated him, so that he would move to Boston and became a leader of his people."

She tapped his wrist with her fan. "Stephen dearest, I have missed you so. Are you going to the soldier lottery!"

"Yes. And you?"

"At the express invitation of General—" She broke off and this time tapped her own mouth. "*Mon Dieu*, Mary Haines at the edge of an indiscretion! 'Tis all your fault, of course. You have left me to my own resources, deserted me. People take advantage of me because of that. Yes, they do, Stephen. Why is it the only time I ever see you now is when I bump into you by accident? Please do not say to me what is on the tip of your tongue to say."

"And what is that?"

"That you are married. I know very well that you're married. Who would know it better? Other men marry and manage to maintain . . . their little friendships. What harm would it do if you dropped by on occasion to talk?"

He kept silent.

After a moment she said, "Will you come tomorrow night? Just for an hour or so. It's Sunday. We can be quiet together."

He shook his head.

"I hate you."

He kept silent.

"I believe this is your stop," she said.

Glancing out, he noted they had reached only Forty-first Street. He looked back at her. Her expression was unyielding. He smiled, bowed, and, like Lieutenant Frazier, made a premature exit.

Provost Marshal Scobie had done his best to keep the crowd meager, but his best had been insufficient. As Stephen approached the corner of Forty-sixth Street, he saw a swarm of about two hundred or so. Still, despite Charley Scobie's anxieties, it was a good-humored, well-behaved crowd, and the score of police assigned to keep order had little to do besides banter back and forth with friends and neighbors. The crowd was mostly working class, fewer toffs than Stephen had expected. The hour, he surmised. Nine-thirty in the morning had proved a deterrent. Yet they were not unrepresented. Here a beaver, there a velvet lapel, and the occasional gold-headed cane as well. Some ladies, too. Having turned the corner of Forty-sixth Street, Stephen now doffed his own beaver half a dozen times to passengers in parked barouches.

That sector of Third Avenue was a row of new, four-story brick structures—shops and other small businesses on the lower floors, tenements on the upper ones. Number six-seventy-seven was headquarters for the provost marshal. It was flanked on the left by Robert Pettigrew's carriage factory and on the right by Kevin Brody's Saloon. The factory was empty. In the saloon draft beer gushed. Stephen managed to push his way through the crowd. When finally he reached the door, he was recognized by the policeman posted there and passed in. He leaned against the wall for a moment, luxuriating in the relative coolness and quiet. It was a large room. It smelled pungently of fresh paint and was decorated . . . festooned, rather . . . with pictures of Abe Lincoln and union flags, both in varying sizes. A wooden railing divided the room in two. Behind the railing, the provost marshal himself and a pair of his subordinates were preparing the huge oaken drum from which twenty-five hundred names would eventually be drawn.

The work was not not going well. Something was wrong with the spinning handle. Snappishly, Provost Marshal Scobie issued a variety of orders. His underlings leaped to obey. But either the orders were counterproductive or the underlings inept. At any rate very little of a positive nature was happening. Someone opened the door. Much of the waiting crowd squeezed in. As Stephen, in advance of it, clambered over the railing, he heard a voice just behind him say, "Is this how Greeley treats a managing editor? Makes him do his own leg work?"

The voice belonged to a short, sixtyish gentleman with a swarthy complexion, one alert blue eye (the other glass), and a repertoire of nervous mannerisms involving his hands, nose, and ears that sometimes drove strangers wild. He was James Gordon

Bennett, publisher of the New York *Herald* and no stranger to Stephen. They were old antagonists—the kind that grow to know each other so well, in fact, that strict attention is required to keep them from becoming friends.

"Told you years ago you should have come with the *Herald*," he said. "You would have owned it by now."

"Humbug."

Bennett's dark intense face creased in a smile. "Well, perhaps. Still, you should have come, you know. You don't even like Greeley."

"At the time I did not like you, either."

"That's true, isn't it? I had forgotten."

But by now Bennett had lost interest in the conversation. His glance had been gauging the crowd.

"Jolly enough," he said.

Stephen nodded.

Across the room was another clutch of reporters. Stephen saw Morrison and Busby from his own paper, and at least three from the *Times*. Kirby was there from Bennett's paper. Kirby waved at them.

"Jolly or not," Bennett said, "they confront one with the disproportionateness of things. So many of them, so few of us. And fewer of us than usual, may I remind you. Except for some wretched pieces of General Macklin's home guard, the military is all up at Gettysburg trying to catch Lee before he gets back across the Potomac. The police? Were you about to mention the police?"

Stephen kept silent.

Bennett took him to task anyway. "My dear sir, at full strength the metropolitan police number two thousand. Eight hundred fifty thousand is our current population, in case you were in doubt."

"I wasn't," Stephen said.

Bennett dug fingers into his scalp. "Difficult days these are, young Jardine. About to become more so." He looked again, assessingly, at the crowd. "In that long ago era when Greeley and

40

I were on speaking terms, he once said to me he thought this city might be better off as its own republic. I told him it was too small."

"It is."

"Yes," Bennett said, drawing down on a lobe as if to separate it from the ear major, "too small for a republic, too large for a lunatic asylum. Or perhaps I am wrong about that. We'll see. We'll see." He shrugged. "Enjoyed your piece yesterday on Boss Tyrell. It was yours, was it not?"

Stephen nodded.

"Knew it. Said to myself—good for young Jardine. He retains the honest man's capacity for shock at the sight of blatant corruption. I, on the other hand, am no longer quite honest or at all shockable."

"I know," Stephen said, smiling.

"Still, I did like the thought of Tyrell a'squirm. Be warned though, young Jardine. He's dangerous, dangerous as a cobra and as self-willed as I am. Which means he'll do you harm if he can. You and the chief inspector. But I suppose you know that, too."

"Yes."

At last the crank was fixed, and a general cheer went up, signaling as much. The drum was now in working order. The first draft in the history of the United States was about to begin, and as Provost Marshal Scobie adjusted the blindfold to cover the eyes of Frank Carpenter, his chief clerk, a certain degree of appropriate tension settled over the room. But not an inordinate amount. The conversational buzz did not die down entirely. And to his left, Stephen heard one man complaining irritably about the heat and another about a horse that had cost him money in a race at Brooklyn Heights the previous morning.

George Southwick, the provost marshal's second clerk, was a short, fat man in his fifties—ruddy-faced normally but not today. Today his face was pale except for the spots over each cheekbone that gleamed like red pennies. His nervousness was painfully apparent. As he inched forward to turn the crank, his knees and belly trembled. This infuriated the provost marshal.

41

"Damn it, man, turn the bloody crank," he roared. "Do it now.!"

From the crowd: "George's scairt. He thinks it's gonna be him goes for a sojer."

"If Georgie Southwick goes for a sojer, the Rebs have had it."

And: "Move it, Georgie." "Get the lead out, Georgie." "Turn the bloody crank, Georgie."

Finally, he did.

The wheel spun. Now a true hush fell on the crowd for the first time, a silence heavy as canvas. The realization seemed to have struck home. Men were about to be conscripted into the army, taken from their homes, families, jobs, saloons. Taken from all that was familiar to them. Lives were about to be changed dramatically, some ended abruptly: "It could be me." "It could me be."

It was William Jones.

William Jones, Forty-sixth Street, corner of Tenth Avenue, became the first man to be conscripted into the United States Army.

And he was on the premises, not twenty feet from Stephen. A man in his early twenties, fair-skinned with blond hair losing to bald and a handlebar mustache that looked too old for him. He smiled disconcertedly at the cheer that went up when the provost marshal called his name. Men close to him pounded his back and shoulders.

"Pack up your carpetbag, Willie."

"Watch out, Rebs, here comes our Willie."

"March to glory, Willie."

From a squat, broad-shouldered woman with a scarlet apron and a blunt, black cigar in her mouth: "Here's a kiss for you, Willie. Come back safe, and God knows what I'll give ya."

Squeaks and giggles from her sisters. Roars of approval in general, subsumed into an extemporized chorus, just a shade drunken:

> "Take your gun and go, Will. Take
> your gun and go. For Ruth can drive
> the ox, Will. And I can use the hoe."

42

But then as the song faded raggedly, a lone voice from the rear added a coda: "You're a dead un, Willie."

His smile disappeared. It was replaced by an expression Stephen thought of as complicated and unsettling. Not fear exactly, but with fear as an element. It was as if William Jones, conscript, was now realizing that something too large for his experience was looming up at him, something too cumbersome to cope with.

"Ain't goin' for no sojer," he roared out suddenly.

Fiercely, he tore himself away from the press around him—hands, hands stretching, reaching almost superstitiously to touch him—and battled his way to an exit.

Bennett said, "Smart lad. I think he's terrified."

"I wish I were young enough," Stephen said before he could stop himself.

Bennett looked at him for a moment and then said, "Of course you do. And of course the first ball fired in your vicinity would take your head off."

By noon, when the provost marshal called an adjournment until Monday morning, Willie Jones had one thousand two hundred thirty-six fellows—among them a councilman named James Bloodworth, half a dozen John Smiths, a sprinkling of John Does, Richard Roes, and one Jesus Christ.

Bennett, having grown restless, did not stay for the entire proceedings. But as he left he said, "You do me good, Jardine. You always do. Why did we once detest each other so?"

"We were ambitious men," Stephen said. "Now only one of us is."

"You?"

"What nonsense."

"Me? Ambitious to be what?"

"President, of course."

Bennett's mouth tightened, and for a moment Stephen thought he was in for the kind of Bennettesque squall he remembered from the old days. But the spasm passed.

"You have the wrong publisher, my friend. Greeley wants to be president. This publisher wants only peace."

Stephen studied him. "Perhaps I was wrong," he said.

Bennett nodded. "But I think neither of us will get what we want," he said, and left.

The crowd broke up, many of its components straggling into Brody's to consider—lengthily and liquidly—the day's events. Excited, yes. Aware that they had participated in history-making scenes, but apparently nothing beyond that, Stephen thought. Then, queasy stomach and aching head notwithstanding, he got back on an omnibus returning to Printing House Square, where Greeley was waiting to hear his report.

Lieutenant Frazier saw him go. "An interesting man that, *n'est-ce pas?*" he said to his companion.

"Is he?" Mary said. "It would never occur to me to think of him in just that way."

"How do you think of him?"

"As a man one could trust with one's life."

2

Unlike the Third Avenue traffic, the Fifth Avenue traffic moved at an opulent crawl. No omnibuses, no wagon carts, no nervous phaetons, the carriages, for the most part, were sedately black. Highly polished, they glistened in the sun. Inside one of these, John Brautigan was trying not to put his large grip on Rosie Shannon's slender shoulders. In characteristic fashion she was leaning too far out the window. She was doing it to tease him. He knew that.

"All the dandies and their giggling belles," Rosie said, finally drawing herself back in. "And my heavens, the finery. You'd hardly know there was a war on."

Brautigan nodded.

"It's nice you have your own carriage, John," she said, caressing the smooth leather. "It's one of the things I like best about you."

Rosie—redheaded, deep brown eyes, lightly freckled and beneath that skin as white as the cross straps on his dress uniform. His Rosie—strong-minded, high-spirited, and alight with a thoroughbred's courage. She was the kind who would have made herself pick up a snake if that's what she was most afraid of. To him she was beautiful beyond description—and such a child.

"It's not my carriage," he said, aware that he spoke too soberly, wishing he could banter with her the way Michael could. "It's the department's, and you know it."

"And are you not the department, Chief Inspector John Brautigan?"

"No, I am not."

She smiled. "Tell your man to stop so we can walk."

He gave the order, and before he could help her out she leaped. Skirts swirling—no constricting hoops for Rosie—she ran up the path that led to the woods surrounding the lovely new park. Unhurriedly—hurry was a thing as unnatural to him as deliberation was to her—he followed. It took him a while to catch up to her. When he did he found her perched on a rock, her vivid green gown daringly hiked above white-stockinged ankles. It was a piece of intentional provocation. He chose not to comment. After a moment she patted the rock's flat surface and shifted over to make room for him. He eased himself down next to her.

"It's a fine park, John, isn't it?" She leaned back, bracing herself on her arms and gazing skyward. "Central Park. I never thought they'd do it well, seeing that this is New York and seeing how your friend Tyrell has his thieving paws into everything."

"My *friend?*"

She laughed.

It delighted him. It catapulted him: "Rosie . . ."

"What is it, Chief Inspector?" she asked, taking his hand.

He caught himself by the coattails and hauled himself back. "Nothing," he said.

She flushed under her freckles with the quick bright flush pretty red-haired people have. "Nothing is a lie," she said.

And he swore inwardly, berating himself for being the inept liar that he was.

"John, you're enough to try to patience of a saint. I wasn't going to . . . I promised myself not to . . . *Why* are you so afraid? John Brautigan, the living scourge of the sixth ward. When he

46

comes swaggering up East Broadway swinging his locust stick all the plug-uglies get to shaking. And yet here am I the merest slip of a girl, and he's terrified."

"Ah, Rosie."

"Rosie what?"

"Nothing."

"Again nothing. Nothing to be *shy* about certainly, for heaven knows I've made it clear how willing I am."

"I'll go to my grave grateful for that, but the question is—"

"Don't. Please don't tell me again about the great disparity in our ages. A person would think you're ready now for that grave you're going to so gratefully."

He looked at her for a long moment, knowing he would never again want anyone the way he wanted her. Words to express this fought for freedom, and a part of him was their willing collaborator. In the end, as always, they were quelled. And as always he could not have said whether wisdom or cowardice had prevailed.

"We will have to be getting back soon," he said heavily. "The supervisor wants me to look in on Provost Marshal Scobie."

"The draft," she said as if the words were medicine. And he thought later that if he'd had the sense he was born with he would have bitten his tongue to keep from saying what he did next. Because any damn fool should have been able to predict how one thing would lead to another.

"Michael was there today," he said.

She made no comment.

"We didn't speak." He paused. "Have you seen him?"

"Yes. He's fine." For a moment it seemed that would be all. Clearly she meant it to be. But the glass was too full; a little spilled over. "Michael's always fine."

"There's some mail come for him at the house. If you—"

"Damn Michael. And damn the mail that's come for him."

"Rosie, don't be like that."

"Michael. Michael. Do we ever really talk about anything else? No, we do not. If suddenly in the midst of this blistering summer

47

day it would begin to snow, you would not pause a moment to wonder at the mystery of it. You would say I hope Michael has his bloody big boots on."

He smiled.

"Don't you laugh at me, John Brautigan. It's true."

"It's not true. What good does it do to make up stories? I'm his father, yes. That doesn't mean I'm blind to his faults."

"As nears as matters."

"I'm not. I know he can be selfish—"

"Do you? Do you know how close he is to the world's championship?"

She had become a statue. He stared at her. He tried to will her back to life. She remained marble. Until, jarringly, she said, "I want to go now. And I don't think we better be seeing so much of each other any more."

She moved away from him. He tried to pull her back, but she eluded him. She hurried down the path. Miserably, he plodded after her. When he reached the carriage she was already in it. He gave instructions to the driver and climbed in next to her, careful not to touch her. She, too, was careful, squeezing over to her side as far as possible, making much of how important it was that her gown not graze his uniform.

The day seemed less pleasant now, hotter, more typically July. Now he felt each rivulet of sweat under his uniform collar. He felt each of his two hundred twenty pounds; each of his years. And as for the park—with its rambling paths, graceful fountains and satiny lawns—he was happy to leave it behind.

The silence between them gained in portent. Things could break under a silence like this, he knew. He longed to be someone else. Someone with a dancing tongue. Someone who could make a girl laugh. But he was no more than himself, only himself.

The shiny black carriage clip-clopped its way over the Fifth Avenue until it reached Twenty-first Street. At this intersection it turned right toward Gramercy Place and the home of the Jardines. Two small boys flung rocks at the carriage. One missed entirely, the other just grazed the fender. If John Brautigan had not

48

been sunk in misery, would he have noticed something odd about these boys? It was a smallish thing, but Brautigan was both a knowing policeman and himself a product of his city's streets. Would he have noticed, then, how remarkably unhurried was their retreat?

3

"Give it here, Michael Brautigan, me bucko, and I'll put a head on it," Police Commissioner Robbo Royce said, but he did not wait to be obeyed. He grabbed the still half-full schooner and took it to the keg for replenishing. He returned it, then moved off to perform the same service on the other side of the campfire.

Michael wished he were a better drinker than he was. Half a schooner and his head was already buzzing. He wished he could really hold his liquor. No man, he knew, could hope to make it to the top in Tammany Hall without having a truly first-rate capacity. Like the commissioner. Or Boss Tyrell. Or, for that matter, like his own father when the mood was on him.

"*Grüss Gott*," a male voice shouted and was followed by a chorus of female giggles.

Michael turned so that he could see the German tumblers leap and twirl and in general conduct themselves as if the temperature were not still—at twilight—hovering around eighty.

The big yellow banner tied between the maple trees read: "Sixth annual Jones Woods gala German-American Liederkranz Festival." And the brass band tootled. The burghers cavorted. The fraus and fräuleins giggled, flirtatiously, Michael thought. And he thought, also, that some of it was directed at him. The lager flowed. Why didn't *they* want to end the draft? Why didn't *they* hate the niggers? Who did they hate instead?

Actually, Michael knew why the German-Americans were less exercised about the draft than the Irish-Americans. The explanation was simple. It was a matter of three hundred dollars. Most of the former could come up with it and thus buy an exemption. To do the same, most of the latter would need leprechauns.

God how he hated being poor. All his life he'd been poor. Not dirt poor, of course. *Respectable* poor. Dirt poor was infinitely better. Dirt poor, you didn't care. Dirt poor, you didn't have Nora Brautigan laundering your handkerchiefs every ten minutes, or ironing your shirts into oblivion. Dirt poor, you jut got down in the dirt and scrabbled for whatever was there. Respectable poor never let up. It meant hiding. And pretending. And living out of the Blanchard charity box.

Things had changed after the chief-inspectorship, but not enough to erase the bitterness of memory—what it had meant to be the only day boy, the only Blanchard scholarship boy at the Hamilton School. Once Michael had tried to convey how that had shriveled him. His father had shrugged and said, "Poor's unpleasant, but it's not fatal, Michael, now is it?"

And of course his father knew, had been a Blanchard boy at Hamilton before him. As had Joe, though for only thirty-seven days.

Michael shuddered. Because he was into it now. Just like that, he had done it to himself. Or the beer had done it. Made no difference. He was trapped now. For a moment he tried to fight back the images. Useless. Always useless. Once loose, they slithered past all defences. Gained ghostly speed and ran their course.

Joe's dead face. The sheet coming up to cover it. And—with almost no break in her motion—his mother turning to scream her

51

litany: "Your fault, John Brautigan. Yours. Yours." His father in
the doorway, silent under the onslaught.

Joe had been seven when the cholera cut him down. And
Michael six, with no keys for decoding his mother's hysteria. Or
for perceiving that his father's fault lay solely in being a yard short
of the apartment door when Death struck.

Later Nora had asked her husband's pardon. And an older
Michael had been able to bring perspective to bear. But forgive?
That was another matter entirely. It was easy enough to pay lip
service to the idea that cholera was cholera and Death, Death after
all. On the other hand, there was the prodigious figure of John
Brautigan. Magical, mythical. Every boy on Michael's block was
awed by him, envied Michael his claim to him. What if he had
been there—and not in Brooklyn extraditing some meaningless
prisoner—might not Death have been given pause? Easier ways to
fill a quota, Death might have said, and moved along to a less
problematical door. And then Joey would have been allowed to
recover and grow up. And Michael, too, would have been allowed
to grow up . . . grow up Michael.

He shuddered again. But the worst was over now. In a practiced
way he waited for calm. It came in a minute or so, and then,
sighing, he took a careful, very careful sip from his schooner.

From across the fire someone called to him, offering him an ear
of roasted corn. He declined. Someone else taunted him with
persnickitiness. He was used to that. He did not even bother to
answer.

Now his glance surveyed his compatriots, the fifteen men and
women who formed a rough circle around the fire. They were
baking potatoes or roasting corn, or drinking from schooners or
flasks, or simply staring into space. They were a joyless group, it
seemed to him, his Irish-American brethren. Apathetic and sullen, compared to that lively group of tootlers and oompahers
across the field. Only thirty yards away, but it was as if they
inhabited another country, the country of the full wallet.

He became aware that Royce was studying him. Instantly, he

fixed his blue-eyed, eager-to-please Irish-American mask in place.

"Shift over," Royce said.

The commissioner was fat and in his late forties, but he looked older. Of medium height, he sagged when he stood and stooped when he walked, his large head hanging forward like an elephant's. His eyes were a boozer's red. Obediently, Michael shifted to accommodate him. There was considerable rump involved, and he was left with but an insecure purchase at the end of the bench.

"Got time for a bit of a parlay, Michael?"

"Yes, sir."

"Robbo. Robbo to you, lad. You're among the anointed, don't you know that? All the big chiefs in the Tammany wigwam, we have admiring eyes on you. And you so young. How old are you, Michael?"

"Nineteen."

A nod, followed by narrow-eyed scrutiny of extended length. "Shall I be honest with you? I mean I wouldn't take the trouble if it wasn't you were a coming man. I mean I would not take an interest. And neither would Tyrell."

"Tyrell takes an interest?"

Royce leaned forward to tap Michael's knee. "But I'll tell you what has him concerned. Can you guess?"

"No."

"Faith, sure you can."

"No. I swear, Robbo."

"Why your old man, of course. Now listen to me, lad. Big John Brautigan's a friend of mine. You didn't know that? Well, I promise you he is. Him and me and Tyrell, all three of us raised on Chrystie Street. Kids together. And, as you well know, Big John and me, we serve on the metropolitans together, the both of us. So there ain't many that's been closer to him through the years than Robbo Royce. And I respect him. You believe that, Michael?"

"Yes."

"And true it is. But it don't signify a tinker's damn because Tyrell and him's like Kilkenny cats. Ain't that the fact of it?"

"I guess so."

Royce smiled. "You know so. Everybody in the two wards knows so." He paused. "The rumor is you've had a split with your old man, that you've moved out on him. That right, Michael?"

"It is."

"Some say, though, you've had them before. And that like as not you'll move back before too long."

"I've been out of his house for three months, Robbo."

"Have you now?"

"And I won't be going back."

More narrow-eyed scrutiny, ending this time in a smile of acceptance. "We're a body short in the Golden Tiger. How'd you like to join us?"

Michael's mind dazzled him with pictures. The parade last May Day. Masses of celebrants lining the street to cheer their favorites. Up Broadway comes the nonpareil, no other fire company like it. A crew of heroes, dragging their legendary engine. Bedecked with all the flowers of spring, it glitters gloriously in the sun. And Tyrell leads the way—Tyrell in a tall beaver hat, a white fireman's coat slung over his arm, his shiny silver talk-trumpet swinging at his side. Oh God, to be part of it all. To join Tyrell's swashbucklers and become one with the seventy-five brothers who manned the famous Golden Tiger. To sew that unique saber-toothed emblem on the right arm of his shirt and wear Tyrell's colors for all the envious world to see.

For all the world to see.

His smile died.

"What's wrong, Michael?" Royce asked.

"I know why he wants me. He wants to score off my father. He wants everybody in the two wards to see John Brautigan's son with Tyrell's brand on him. That's the reason, the only reason."

Royce drained his lager and wiped his mouth with the back of his hand. He went to the keg, returning when his schooner was filled.

54

"Tyrell wouldn't know I was alive if it wasn't for John Brautigan being my dad," Michael said and kicked a pebble.

"Will I tell Tyrell no thanks then?"

Michael looked glum.

"Waiting, lad."

"Can I think on it?"

Royce raised his eyebrows.

"Tomorrow. No later, Robbo. I promise."

"Well, all right. But no later because . . ." Purposefully, he glanced around at their compatriots who sat in self-contained islands of two and three. Then, leaning forward so that he could whisper, he said, "Because there are careers and careers." He paused. "Tyrell sees it something like this. First, the Brotherhood of the Golden Tiger. Assistant foreman next year. Foreman the year after that. And then within five years . . . well, the fact is, Michael, love, Tyrell sees you as an alderman."

Michael's throat went dry, but before he could comment, Bridget Murphy suddenly shouted, "I'm tired of hanging about, Royce. They coming, or ain't they?"

"Yeah," Pat Murphy said, standing to glare more effectively.

And from Dennis Murphy: "They coming, or ain't they?"

The Murphys often spoke as a family group—Bridget leading it off, husband and son in counterpoint. Bridget was about fifty. She had the tan leathery skin of a gypsy and the faded blue eyes of a cynic. She was tall and angular, taller than her husband but not taller than her son. That was fitting, since she looked down on the former and worshipped the latter. Both men accepted these responses as reasonable.

Royce struggled erect, reached into his watch pocket, then peered across the sward. He saw only German celebrants.

"Right," he said, "let's get started. Gather in closer, my friends."

They did, maintaining their sets. It was as if each little group wished to underscore its territorial integrity. They were not a mass, they seemed to be saying. They might well have mutual objectives, but they would approach these as chieftains represent-

55

ing definable constituencies. Sixth and seventh ward people were counting on them to do that.

Michael backed off and found a seat some five yards away, as far from the Murphys as he could get and still stay within hearing. He thought of the Murphys as subhuman. Almost everyone did, including Boss Tyrell, who, when he employed them did so not despite but because of that.

Royce mopped his brow. Then, half a beat before anyone in his audience was ready for it, he thundered, "Bridget Murphy, do you want your man to die for a nigger?"

The German band stopped playing. As if Royce's thunder had been some kind of dread signal, the Leiderkranz Festival was collectively folding its tent. It was probably not true the Germans were fleeing in terror. Probably the agreed upon closing time had been reached, but it was funny to see them skedaddle.

Bridget never got to answer Royce's question. Three figures had suddenly materialized on the circle's perimeter—two well-known, one a stranger. And it was the stranger who answered. "If we're a brotherhood, none of us need die for the niggers," he said.

Though it carried easily, his voice was soft. It was also unmistakably southern. He was tall with long white hair that came to his shoulders—striking, since he was no more than forty. Fair-skinned. A mustache that curled flamboyantly at the ends: white horns. He wore a white linen suit, no weskit, no hat. His cane was ruby-headed. He carried it in such a way as to lead Michael to believe it was one of those that encased a sword.

The ladies stirred.

"Who the hell's he?" a man wanted to know.

This was Frank Hennessy. He owned an East Broadway saloon famous for being the sixth ward Saturday night headquarters, which is to say the place where sixth warders got liquored up before searching out seventh warders to bash.

His wife, Peg, was famous for never smiling. She was smiling now.

Royce said, "Friends, I want you to meet Duncan McAusland

56

Campfield of Richmond, Virginia. And the other two gentlemen, of course, need no introduction."

That was certainly true. Terence Tyrell and Liam Devlin. Michael had known of both of them since he was a child. Legendary figures. You could not live on the Lower East Side and escape knowledge of them, though they were no longer, to be sure, of equal standing.

Devlin, sixty and skeletal, had patchy gray-white hair and tiny eyes that had terrified a generation of recalcitrant politicians. He was the seventh ward's leader. Once he had been considerably more. Once had had been the preeminent power in the Tammany structure. Three years ago, however, in a passionate councilmanic confrontation—still recalled wherever Tammany men met to swap aural history—Tyrell had beaten him, toppled him. And having done so, patronized him by allowing him his smidgen of status. Tubercular—and growing worse—Devlin was something of a recluse these days. When he was seen at all, it was usually the harbinger of a fateful occasion.

Tyrell: the trademark girth, the shiny black beard that spread down over it. When he laughed—he was laughing now—his mountainous belly threatened avalanche. It was a laugh that commanded attention. Michael was swept up in it, laughing with Tyrell and believing with all his heart that the Boss, who owned the city now, would soon own the state, and that the country must fall to him as a matter of course.

"Listen to the man," Tyrell said, beaming, jabbing affectionately at Campfield's arm. "When he talks about brotherhood, he's talking about being your brother. And my brother. And all of us brothers banding together and doing ourselves some good."

"Maybe he's your brother, Tyrell," Hennessy said, "but no damn southern dandy was ever mine. My brother never wore a white suit in his life."

There were some snickers at this—none of them female, Michael noticed.

"Don't make a gnat's ass of a difference about suit color. Hell, no, Frank. Ain't suit color that matters, it's *skin* color."

57

"Yes, gentlemen," Campfield said, "That is exactly what matters. All white men are my brothers. And our common enemy is the nigger. Who if he isn't stopped will take your jobs first. And when he's got that, he'll take your houses. And when he's got that, he'll run you out of the streets on which you live. And when he's done that . . ." He paused for effect. "He'll take your women."

Breaths sharply indrawn.

"Oh, yes, brothers," Campfield said, "I have seen it happen. I can tell you stories. Brothers, the stories I could tell you: black buck niggers taking our women so their pickaninnies can come out a little less sable."

And then Bridget Murphy leaping to her feet, eyes wild, screamed, "By Christ, I'll tell you a story here and now. No man of mine's going to get his arse shot off for the sake of some dirty, raping nigger."

Royce: "That's fighting talk, Tammany kind of talk."

Tyrell: "A band of brothers."

Campfield: "Brothers, hear me. Are you listening to me, brothers? If we act like brothers, we can turn back the black hordes."

"Burn," said Devlin suddenly.

And so it went. They spent the next few hours tapping the keg, passing the jug, exciting each other and making plans. These took various shapes. For a while they talked of kidnapping Provost Marshal Scobie. This was superceded by the kidnapping of Mayor Gibbons, an idea that found considerable favor since Gibbons was a Republican and by definition despicable.

Into every pause, however, Devlin said, "Burn." He was ignored at first by the more commonsensical among them, who, at this point, were also the more vocal. But as dusk changed to dark, and the fire around which they were gathered grew fuller, richer, and at the same time more ominous, Devlin became in a sense their keynoter. Still, demonstration—that only—was what they finally agreed on: protest. Mobilize at Scobie's office, show 'em all they meant business. The city fathers, the black Republicans, Mayor Gibbons and his henchmen must be moved to take the will of the people seriously, Tyrell informed them. At around nine o'clock

58

they began to leave, rendezvous points established. And by nine-thirty only Michael remained, staring into the fire. He thought about what had been said—not so much to them but to him—and what it implied. He sat there for an hour, hearing Tyrell's voice, listening to it as if it were a siren's.

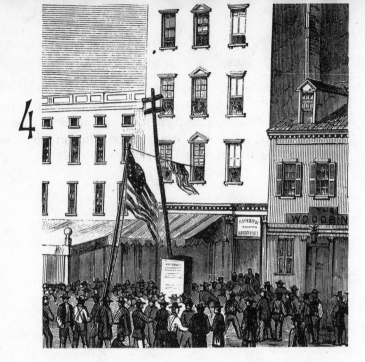

4

From Stephen Jardine's diary. Saturday, July 1:

. . . Greeley, apple in one hand, a copy of Bennett's *Herald* in the other: "Do you see what that cad writes about me? I mean Bennett, your friend. The scoundrel writes that I'm an abject coward. And a liar as well. That I have a secessionist flag hidden in my closet, should Jefferson Davis prove victorious. What do you say to that, Jardine?"

"That it sounds to me like something you wrote about him last week."

Storms from my office. Fifteen minutes later, sends a graceful note reiterating his destestation of Bennett but apologizing for his loss of temper. I sent one in return thanking him for the apology. I should have those printed in mass.

Also, he wished to inform me of a secret meeting to be held at the St. Nicholas Hotel tomorrow. Called by Mayor Gibbons. Its purpose is to discuss the draft situation in general and specifically what if anything should be done by the city's Respectable Persons in response to it. Having informed me of the meeting, he then ordered me not to go near it. Greeley takes the position that there is no situation, thus no response is required.

But there *is* a situation. Governor Spencer knows there is a situation. According to pressroom rumor, his response to it is a tactical vacation somewhere in the Jersey pine barrens. In the pressroom they say men in high places are behind much of the unrest. "Southrons"—Northerners with Southern sympathies. People who, for a variety of reasons, have opposed the war from the outset. Governor Spencer, for instance.

And down in the lower wards, they know there is a situation. Tyrell, that spider, is at work there plotting. Spinning webs in behalf of Tammany's Democrats. Which is to say in behalf of himself.

John Brautigan stopped by a while ago, and though he would not be pumped I could tell he, too, thinks we are in for squally weather. He, too, has been parading the wards.

And I could tell also, though he spoke even less of that, how much Michael preys on his mind. Michael. Strange to think I once held him on my knee. Beautiful and quick, that was small Michael. So much quicker than small Joe. But it was Joey you wanted to hug for his sweetness.

John, old friend, where have the years taken us? Does it seem so long ago to you that we wore our Hamilton freshman caps into the bleakness of Blanchard Hall? And were caned, *seriatim*, for trying to flee from it? You, because your mother was dying and that idiot house proctor, Danielson, would not give you leave to go—me, yielding to a tiger-spring of homesickness. Mutually afflicted, we swore brotherhood.

All is quiet in my house now. Margaret sleeps. *My* son, bless him, does likewise. Only the master is wakeful.

We are quarreling just now, Margaret and I. I accused her this morning, not for the first time, of bringing "the great cause" into our house, which puts her in the position of preaching to the converted since I am already a believer in the rights of women. Not for the first time, she accused me of a less than fervent

61

conversion, of frequent backsliding. And the truth, as always, is that neither Jardine is skilled at viewing objectively.

What a pointless exercise this is. An exercise in insomniacal futility. The fact is, Jardine, you adore her, as helplessly as ever old Henry Blanchard did. And if she is at times autocratic and Blanchardy, she is also at times remarkably the opposite. And a brave and passionate fighter for her cause. And with that a far better mother than she credits herself to be.

The fact is I love what Margaret has wrought here, the life she has made for me. It is not anything I could have imagined when we were youngsters, the three of us, and I was so certain she would one day belong to Peter.

I remember the day . . . *the* day. My father and I are breakfasting together, hurriedly, for a note has been sent to our door, and soon he must leave to deliver his . . . what? . . . thousandth child? His black bag is on the table. Through the window I can see Enoch holding the carriage horses. Another carriage draws up. Margaret leaps from it, handkerchief to her eyes. My father looks at me. He wants to know if he should stay. I shake my head. How indelibly all this is printed on my mind. How old was I? Thirty. Peter a year older. Margaret just twenty-one.

Margaret: I am going to Paris.

Me: What has Peter done to you?

She looks daggers and will not answer. And to this day hasn't. And a week later off she goes to study painting, to test the extent of her talent, she has told us all. And there she stays for two talent-testing years. During which life goes on. The practice Peter shares with my father flourishes. Greeley and I find that, appearances to the contrary, there are ways in which we are compatible. (Mary Haines and I make a similar discovery.) And finally Margaret signals it was a modest talent after all.

She returns. But the ancient basis is obviously altered. They avoid each other. Incomprehensibly, Peter avoids *me*. One night, however, I track him down. We talk, drink. I say to him, "I want her, do you?" And he has the temerity to make a joke. I kick the table over. (I do believe I kicked him, too, when he tried to rise,

62

drenched as he was in the Madeira we had been sharing.) Still enraged, I march to Governor Blanchard's house, hammer at the door (fortunately, he is from home), fight past three servants on my way to Margaret's room, which I never reach. We meet midpoint on the stairs—she in her nightdress; me draped in servants. She dismisses them. Wipes my bloody nose. Kisses my yearning mouth. Calls me dearest.

And then for seven years she fills this house with joyous things. With attractive, intelligent people who tolerate me at first for her sake but later achieve something like affection for me, I do believe, quirky as I am. And then the child is born. I have a family. And dear God, how empty my life would be without it all. How grateful I am to you, Margaret. And having written the above, and meant it with all my heart, what do I do if it becomes clear— unavoidably, inescapably—that you have been false?

Sunday
July
2,
1863

Frazier knew she didn't like him.

For her brother's sake, she was trying hard to be civil, but the antipathy crept out here and there—in a bitten off word, or in a smile too forced. It was difficult to blame her. He felt one way about things, she another, and if there was a middle ground, it was hard to see where it lay. He tried to shrug it off. He'd been sent here to do a job . . . a difficult job . . . a job he believed in . . . and he was the picked man for it. Selected because he'd earned his reputation for single-mindedness and devotion to duty. Well, then, let him get on with it.

"Nathaniel asked that I give you coffee while you wait," she said. "He won't be long. Won't you come into the kitchen."

"In a moment," he said.

The house was small and trim, the way she herself was. Two bedrooms and a little sitting room. A large bookcase made it seem even smaller. He saw Shakespeare there; Dryden, Dunne, Washington Irving, and of course the sturdy theological standbys so familiar to him as the backbone of his father's library. But he saw nothing by his father, or Frederick Douglass, or any of the other black radicals. He was not really surprised. He suspected that Reverend Dawson's militancy—such as it was—was of recent vintage. He was the kind of black man who had spent his life yearning to be white. And many were the peas in that particular pod, especially among the educated. But it was changing— everywhere and fast, Frazier thought with satisfaction.

A clean brown carpet covered the floor and six wooden chairs circled a good dark walnut table. The table looked expensive. It also looked lovingly cared for. On the mantle were photographs of the younger Dawsons and two dignified older folks, the progenitors. Like Frazier's own father, the older Reverend Dawson had been a slave, and through a combination of good fortune, endless effort, and hard, mean scrimping had put together enough money to buy his freedom.

"Will they be at the church?" he asked. "Your parents?"

"They would have been. They never missed Nathaniel's preaching. But they're dead. My father just last year."

"Yes," he said, having recalled that a moment too late. "My father said so. I'm sorry."

Next to the photographs was an array of bright, painted coffee mugs—a variety of motifs. Some merely designs, others scenes of plantation life, and still others faces—both black and white— caricatures mostly, all done with style and wit and virtually all in good nature. One was not. It was a white man. The cruelty in his face was naked. Clearly, it was out of place among these others. He wondered if it had been left there by mistake.

"Did you do these?" he asked, indicating the body of the work.

She nodded.

He hesitated, then lifted the misfit. "This, too?"

She took it out of his hand. "Lieutenant Frazier, your coffee will be getting cold."

He noticed that she did not restore the mug to its former place. Instead it disappeared into the cupboard. On their way to the kitchen they passed the open door of a bedroom—white sheets and pillows and a bright patchwork quilt. Immaculate. He guessed it was hers, and that behind the closed door of the larger bedroom the Reverend Dawson was putting the finishing touches on his sermon. He felt an unexpected pang of homesickness. At this very moment the Reverend Frazier must be putting the finishing touches on his. The kitchen was blatantly scoured, the table set for one only. He was not surprised.

"I'd be pleased, Sister Cora, if you'd join me," he said.

"No, thank you. We breakfasted hugely, my brother and I. And now I really must attend to chores."

"Can't they wait?"

"They've waited so long now—"

He smiled. "What you mean is your brother asked you to give me coffee, but he didn't specifically say you had to stay in the room while I drank it."

Her skin was darker than his—a shade—but just light enough to show a blush. She had large, liquid creole eyes, desperately unwilling to meet his.

"Do you really dislike me so?" he asked.

She sighed. "Please sit, Lieutenant Frazier."

He did and watched while she poured the steaming fluid into two cups. It smelled delicious. He realized then with sudden sharpness that he was hungry and was pleased when thick brown buttered bread was heaped on a plate next to him.

"It's not you I dislike," she said, sitting. "It's the uniform."

"What's wrong with the uniform?"

"It stands for killing."

He took a sip of the coffee before replying. "Your brother wouldn't put it that way."

"That's because he's been seduced."

He laughed, but she continued as though he hadn't.

"My brother, though young, is almost always a clearheaded man. He would not be behaving so savagely had not some form of seduction taken place."

"I see."

"Nathaniel is valued in this city not only for Christian leadership, but for his judgment in all matters. I do not exaggerate, Lieutenant."

"Valued by whom?"

"By his brothers, of course. But by people of the white race, too."

"You mean because he's a good nigger?"

She took a deep breath, but kept silent.

"Sister Cora," he said, "I think those white ladies who eddicated you done eddicated the black out of you."

Her chin came up. "And I think you forget yourself, sir."

"Maybe. But the one thing I don't forget is I'm a nigger. And that this pretty blue suit don't make me less a nigger. Just like this pretty little house of yours don't make *you* less a nigger. The sign out there says York Street, not Waverly Place."

"Please don't use that word in this house."

"Nigger? It disturbs you? Well, I don't much like it either. But that don't signify. Because freedman I may be, little sister, which is to say legally. But I ain't free, and you ain't free, and none of us is until all of us is—and the word nigger just don't exist any more. Now your brother understands that. Nobody had to *seduce* him into understanding that. He just naturally does. Why don't you?"

"I understand it, all right. It means killing."

"It means doing what it is needful to do."

"Killing?"

"Yes. If it's needful. And dying, too."

"Oh, I don't mind the dying," she said.

She looked so fierce saying that, and at the same time so fresh and pretty, so young and far from dying, that it made him smile. And that rekindled her anger. She got up and would have fled had he not reached over to hold her back.

"Don't go. Please," he said. "Stay and forgive me for being clumsy."

She hesitated.

"It's only Christian," he said.

She didn't smile. Nor did she speak, but it seemed to him that some of the stiffness had left her shoulders.

"And is this not the Lord's day?" a voice asked. They turned, and saw a short, plump black man standing at the threshhold of

70

the room. Ten years older than his sister, Reverend Dawson narrowed that gap every time he grinned. Which he was doing now, benignly. "Come, Cora, pour me some of your splendid coffee, and let us all be loving together."

As she rose to fill his cup, Frazier watched her. All her movements were compact, neat, so competent, he thought, for one so young. He was pleased at the way she moved. He was pleased when she touched the back of her brother's head affectionately. Everything about her pleased him, he acknowledged, and tried instantly to switch the channel of his thoughts.

There was a knock at the door. Cora went to it, opened it to two men, a vividly ill-assorted pair. From his size, Frazier took the foremost to be a boy. But then he saw the traces of white in his hair and recognized him.

"Come in, come in," Reverend Dawson said. "Don't stand out in that hot sun, brothers. Come into the cool. Cora, find out if our friends will take refreshment."

Protestations from both. Calmly, Cora ignored this, seated them at the table, filled their hands with coffee mugs and then left. In the interim, Reverend Dawson made the one introduction that was necessary. Frazier felt himself stared at appraisingly.

The little man was grinning. "We come to look at the shoulder strap," he said, nodding toward Frazier. "Randy, he don't believe in no nigger shoulder straps."

Suddenly his companion reached over and grabbed Frazier's hand. It was held up so all could see the palm. "This man am a total stranger to hard work. Willie Jones, you going to be waiting the longest day of your life if you expecting me to say this man's a nigger."

"What am I?" Frazier asked.

"A liar." His hand was tossed back to him.

Willie chortled. "Lord, that Randy stubborn as a jackass. He think I'm making it all up about a nigger shoulder strap. He don't want to believe in no nigger shoulder strap because he don't want to believe in nothing higher than a nigger barber."

Despite the white in his hair, Willie was only in his early

71

thirties. The top of his head reached no higher than Frazier's adam's apple, but his chest was powerful, and there was both strength and grace in his walk. Except when he thought he was being observed. Then his gait could become a shamble so complex as to be almost crablike.

"We met last night, didn't we?" Frazier said. "At Mary Haines's."

"Yes, sir."

Frazier nodded, then turned to Randy. "What's your full name?"

"Never give out my full name. That's mine to keep."

Willie said, "Randy the Dandy, his name."

It fit. He wore a white stovepipe hat and a long white coat open to show a brilliantly flowered weskit. Over this could be seen an immense watchguard. His cravat was red. His cane was black with a gleaming silver head. Willie was mundanely, even shabbily dressed. Randy was a picture.

"Better than Nigger Willie, the cathouse piano player," he said mildly. But it was to Frazier he spoke—and then added, "Ain't just me, you know. Nobody, excepting Willie, of course, ever heard of no nigger shoulder strap before. All the black regiments, they got white shoulder straps. Black sergeants, sure. I heard about some of them."

"Randy the Dandy," Willie said. "He our military expert. General Meade, he come to Randy's barber shop every time he in the city just so's the two of them can sit down and talk strategy."

"I got a cousin Samuel—"

"Oh, lordy, lordy, not that same, eternal cousin Samuel."

"My cousin Samuel, he my daddy's brother Ben's boy, come up from near-abouts Atlanta. You hearing me, Lieutenant?"

"I hear you."

"That was back in '61, late part, November, December. He here for awhile, Chicago for awhile, Cincinnati for a while, other places, and always he got one thing in mind. He want to go for a soldier. First, they won't let him. No way they going to let a nigger boy be a soldier. No way. Then when they decide digging ditches and cleaning privies and fetching and carrying in general ain't

72

that much fun, they say to themselves, 'Hey, what we got black boys for?' So they ups and forms these fetching-and-carrying regiments. But no muskets, hear? 'What a nigger want to carry a musket for? To kill secesh? How you going to kill secesh when everybody knows niggers are too scared to fight?' So Samuel, he pretty discouraged. He skip out on the fetching-and-carrying soldiers and come back east again, to Boston this time. And this time things go right for Samuel. Know what I'm working up to tell you, Lieutenant?"

"I think so."

Willie's teeth gleamed. "Me, too. I think so, too. Big test coming up, Reverend. You and me's got to be the judge."

"Cousin Samuel, he wind up in the Fifty-fourth Massachusets, yes he do, Lieutenant. That's the number I see there on your shoulder, ain't it?"

"It is."

"Yes, sir. It look like that to me."

"What is Samuel's full name?"

"Anyways," Randy said, as if Frazier hadn't spoken, "I takes myself up there to Boston where they got the Fifty-fourth of Mass in training, and them darkies is a sure enough pleasure to watch. Smart, quick, slap them muskets, step, turn . . . And when they get to marching, with the band playing and the flags flying . . . my heavens, I done quit this earth all together. White folks watching, they say they never seen nothing like it. I was there two days, and I sure enough did enjoy myself. Too bad I didn't see hide nor hair of you, Lieutenant."

"That's possible, isn't it? Five-six hundred men?"

Randy nodded his head vigorously. "Yes, sir. And it's just as possible that in two days Samuel wouldn't mention a remarkable thing like a nigger shoulder strap, but even poor Willie here wouldn't bet a big part of his poke on it."

"Never you mind what poor Willie would or wouldn't bet his poke on. Let's just wait and see."

"There are four Samuels I know of in the Fifty-fourth," Frazier

73

said after a long moment. "Maybe more. Was your cousin a corporal when you saw him last?"

"A corporal?"

"You ain't deaf," Willie said. "Is he or ain't he?"

"You might say so."

"Samuel Sutton," Frazier said.

Randy kept silent.

Willie, softly, said, "Lordy, lordy."

"Corporal Samuel Sutton was seriously wounded at Port Hudson last week, Randy, did you know that?"

"No, sir, I didn't. How—"

"He took a minié ball in the knee during the initial charge but stayed under fire until forced to the rear. I did the forcing, Randy. When I visited him in the hospital just before I left for here he was mending nicely. Probably he'll be writing soon to tell you that himself."

"Samuel can't write a lick," Randy muttered.

"Then one of his brothers will do it for him. And I expect he'll inform you then that Corporal Sutton has become Sergeant Sutton."

Randy's face brightened. "That's good. Samuel's—"

"A fine man, a brave man. He deserved his promotion. And I think I deserved mine," Frazier said, suddenly grinning. "It came on the same day Samuel's did, and when he informs you of his, he might just say a word about mine. From sergeant to lieutenant."

Willie leaped ceilingward. "Five American greenbacks," he said on coming down, laughing and pounding Randy's back. "Put them here in poor Willie's poke. Ah, a great day. A hallejualiah day. Win five dollars from Randy the miser barber, and it's a day for jubilee."

Glumly, Randy paid off, and while he was doing so Reverend Dawson, sharing at least a portion of Willie's pleasure, rose to take leave of them. "I'll look for you at the church, Lieutenant," he said.

Frazier nodded. "And these?" Indicating Willie and Randy.

74

"I'm afraid they're not churchgoing men, though perhaps you can persuade them. They'd be most welcome."

"Sure is good coffee," Randy said. He took a deep appreciative sniff. "That Sister Cora, she sure do know how to brew an upstanding cup of coffee."

Willie kept silent. Diligently, he was working a piece of leather that had come loose from the sole of his boot. He was trying to rip it off.

Reverend Dawson left.

After a moment Randy said, "He a good man, Reverend Dawson. But he in a line of work never did mean much to me. If there's God, it's a buckra God. And all that God ever done to the nigger is bust his ass."

"Either of you family men?" Frazier asked.

"That's another thing never meant much to me," Randy said. "But Willie here, he had a wife once."

"She done run off," Willie said, still working on his shoe.

"What does mean something to you, Randy?"

He shrugged.

"Your brothers?"

"What brothers? I ain't got no brothers. All I got is myself."

"Willie?"

"You better be careful about your answer, Willie, son," Randy said. "You *know* what the lieutenant working up to."

"What he working up to?"

"He working up to you getting your black ass shot off. You ready to do that?"

Willie looked at Frazier. "I hear tell the first white boy to be drafted yesterday, he named Willie Jones, too. You hear that?"

"It's true. I was there."

"Been thinking about that all last night."

"Why?" Randy asked. "That supposed to mean something? Sometime the dice come up snake-eye twice in a row. What *that* mean?"

"Nothing. Except if I was to join up, that white boy, Willie Jones, he like to be my brother in arms. That right, Lieutenant?"

"Yes."

"But that boy, he don't want to spit on the best part of me. Ain't that so?"

"Does it matter?"

"I'm asking you, Lieutenant."

"How you feel about white trash, how white trash feels about you, none of that matters. All that matters now is what we have to do."

"And if Willie gets himself killed," Randy said. "You going to say to him that don't matter neither."

"Yes. Because it's the truth."

For a moment the silence in the room was electric. Then Willie let his breath out and grinned. "Wrote me a song last night," he said. "Banged it out on the piano at Mrs. Haines's. But I might sing it at the church this morning, Lieutenant, if you was to want me to."

"Damn silly song if you ask me," Randy said and marched to the window to stare out.

"Like for me to sing it to you now?"

"Yes. Please."

"Just the one verse," Willie said. He shut his eyes for a moment, then threw back his head and sang free and easy. He was a powerful baritone and the volume brought Cora to the threshhold of her room.

> "If the devil do not catch
> Jeff Davis, that rebel wretch,
> And roast and fricassee that rebel,
> What's the use of any devil?"

"I sure do like that, Willie," Frazier said.

"That is one damn silly song," Randy said.

"And you will sing it at the church today?"

Willie nodded.

Randy, who had turned to watch, groaned.

"And will you do one thing more?" Frazier asked.

"What's that?"

"Numbskull," Randy said. "You *know* what that is."

"After Reverend Dawson's sermon, he's going to let me speak to the congregation. I'm going to say to the brothers what I said to you just now—about the war. And why it matters that we fight in it. Then I'm going to ask for volunteers. Will you be the first to come forward?"

"I expect so," Willie said. "I expect I been drifting that way ever since I set eyes on you."

Frazier went to him and hugged him. Then, blandly, over his shoulder, he said, "And you, Randy?"

Randy shot him a glance of pure outrage and stamped from the house.

"I better go after him," Willie said. "He gets like this, he gets to drinking, and he gets in trouble. I'll see you at the church in a little while, Lieutenant."

They shook hands and Willie left.

"How long a stay do you plan in our city, Lieutenant?" Cora asked after a moment.

"Only a week. Maybe less. Why?"

"How fortunate for us womenfolk. Two weeks, and you'd have us pared to our lame and halt."

He laughed. It was a curious, silent kind of laugh, but it resonated in a way that left her shaken despite herself.

77

2

The Governor Henry C. Blanchard Asylum for the Benefit of Colored Children in the City of New York had come into being some thirty years earlier because the founder's wife and two of his sisters could not bear it that homeless black babies were placed in jails and poorhouses. Furious, they had swooped down on an offending structure, rescued eleven children in a range of ages and sizes, and marched away with them. That was the beginning. Now, on the Fifth Avenue, the impressive new brownstone, four stories high, covered half a block between Forty-fifth and Forty-sixth streets. Set off by trees, flower beds, vegetable gardens, and a fine green lawn, it was an extremely pleasant place. Much of the credit for this—more than a hundred thousand dollars of her own money had gone into design and reconstruction—belonged to the founder's daughter. And on this particular Sunday, in that briefest of interludes between temperate and torrid, she was now approaching.

"Stop here, Enoch," Margaret Jardine told her driver, on a sudden impulse.

Still fifty yards short of the front gate, he halted instantly. He sat unmoving. Despite this he managed to express perfect displeasure. Enoch, a black freedman in his seventies, had become Margaret's personal driver shortly after her marriage, and though he was used to her erratic stops and starts by now, he far from approved of them. Or her. The radical in Margaret unnerved him. All this gatherin' up to female meetings. All this hullabaloo about what was and what wasn't owed to women. Just not seemly, in Enoch's view.

Without giving much thought to it, Margaret guessed a good bit of what was going on in Enoch's mind. It could hardly surprise her. In a sense male disapproval was a staple of her life, and her mother had prepared her for that a long time ago. She could recall the day. It had been at Seneca Falls, that unforgettable time of the first fully organized women's rights convention.

"They'll never understand you," she had said. "When they give you what you want, it'll be because you've struck the fear of God into them."

Almost fifteen years ago that bright, early fall day. Her mother had seen very few more bright fall days. A week later she had taken to her bed. A month after that she'd been dead of consumption.

Margaret thought then of the only two men she had ever known whose approval had been constant, her father and her husband. And having thought of this she had at least a partial insight into the sudden impulse that had caused her to stop. Damn Peter Mackenzie anyway. What right had he to invade her orphanage, make himself so at home there?

Be fair, she told herself at once. Where was Peter's crime? On indefinite convalescent leave, he was, on the face of it, guilty of nothing more than the useful division of his time between the Metropolitan Hospital and the orphanage. Oh, on the face of it. On the face of it was all well and good unless one knew better. Unless one understood that turmoil was in Peter Mackenzie's nature, that he made trouble as unthinkingly as a child made mudpies.

Turmoil, trouble, emotional bombardments . . . ever since that day when her mother had first taken sick and Doctor Jardine

79

had come to her house, bringing his youthful new associate. She had been fifteen, Peter twenty-five and just back from three years of study in various European medical schools.

How cut-to-the-pattern his behavior that day when one looked back at it. Up, down, North Pole, South Pole . . . in its very immoderation, how much a microcosm of their entire relationship.

Terrified by the evidence her mother tried to hide but could not—each hard cough brought up its own vivid cargo—she had been certain death was minutes away. And he had seen that. No one else had. No one else—not even the Governor—had paid much attention to her that day, but Peter saw the terror in her face. He whispered something to Doctor Jardine. And then, without so much as a by-your-leave, she had been bundled into his carriage and was on her way to St. John's Park.

She would never forget the breakneck speed. Thirty minutes or so and scarcely a word to her, while the pace of his big gray horse kept increasing. Never mind that the road was icy. And that no other carriage on the horizon dared more than the most sedate of crawls. Up a notch, up another until the trees swept by in a snow-laden blur, until a modestly gaited phaeton, going the other way, was passed closely enough for the two vehicles to exchange paint, until the terror gripping her had so little to do with her mother's illness she felt hot with shame.

At last he turned to her, "You've got past the worst," he said cooly and slowed the horse. Mortified, she had wanted to kill. Except he'd been right, of course.

But what did he want from her now? Was it nothing but mischief making? Certainly he was capable of that sort of irresponsibility. Or did he actually believe they could be boy-girl together as if all those intervening years had not happened? Absurd. And Stephen, too, was being absurd. And infuriating. With his watchfulness that he pretended was anything and everything but. Suspecting her of . . . of heaven knew what. All of which, of course, was really what this morning's quarrel had been about. True, the only name mentioned had been Elizabeth

Cady Stanton's, not Peter's, and yet so quickly had they flamed up at each other that both knew, in the coolness of aftermath, that the basis was emotional, not intellectual.

"Mrs. Stanton calls for suffrage now," Stephen had said, setting down his newspaper, "but Greeley is right when he says it's too soon."

"Too soon?" Fairly shrieking. "Not a minute too soon. Mrs. Stanton calls for suffrage because without it we are subhuman. To have drunkards, idiots, ruffians, and illiterates recognized while women are denied is too grossly insulting."

"I speak tactically, damn it."

And so she had sneered at his tactics. Called them overcautious, hinting at worse, and then, before he could reply, had risen from the table, laying dramatic claim to a splitting headache. Blaming him for that, too. He had responded with the suggestion that she pass up her daily visit to the orphanage, earning himself a fresh accusation: insensitivity. To what? Why, to her need to be needed. To be useful, to do something with her vitality. Did he imagine she was some dabbler, some spoony-headed dilettante? No, she was a person of substance. She had value. She was an intelligent, energetic woman with more of a talent for administration than ninety-nine out of a hundred men she knew. And on and on. Oh, it had been outrageous. Accusing Stephen, of all people, of insensitivity. Stephen who practically vibrated when she walked into a room. He had lifted the coffeepot, knuckles whitening on the handle. She thought herself fortunate now that he had not thrown it.

The set of Enoch's shoulders told her that the carriage had been motionless for some few minutes. Sighing, she debarked, glancing upward as she did. From her office window on the second floor two small children waved at her. With her furled parasol she waved back. Peter was between them. He did not wave.

When she reached her office, however, he was alone, still standing before the window. Hearing the door shut, he turned.

"Shiloh," he said. "We made a kitchen table into an operating table, and there I was cutting, hacking, sawing. And soon neat

81

stacks of arms and legs reached to the ceiling." He leaned against the wall, awaiting her reaction.

"That is obscene," she said. "You inflict it on me intentionally."

"Why would I do that?" Holding up his hand before she could answer, he said, "Actually the answer is obvious. Come now, Margaret, you knows the answer as well as I. It is because I love you, my dear. And knowing what a rotter and hopeless cad I am, I want to save you from me by making myself repellent in your eyes."

"I was saved years ago," she said. "I have been in no danger ever since."

He bowed, deeply Teutonic, a heel click to finish it off. Because of his special shoe it would have been clumsy anyway. He made a comedy of it, knowing how this would irritate her.

"Do you have something in particular to discuss with me?" she asked. "If not I have letters to answer, and—"

"Busy, busy Margaret. Has no time for old friends in their misery."

"One old friend per family is sufficient—considering the hard usage you put your friends to."

He smiled. "Poor Stephen. He gave his all last night."

Voice suddenly softer. "Peter, is it your foot?"

"My foot? You mean my lack of foot. No, my dear. Footless or footed, it is all the same."

She marched to her desk and sat down behind it, reaching, as she did, for the foremost of three piles of correspondence, which in diminishing order of priority she had arranged the night before. Impatiently, she said, "You've been drinking."

He ignored that. "It's not lack of foot, you see. It's lack of . . ." He winced. And yet not quite that, she thought. Or more than that perhaps. It was a lightninglike change of expression that had some pain in it, certainly, but just as much anger. Not directed at her, she thought. At least not exclusively, and at any rate gone almost before she had identified it. "Call it lack of worth," he said, now merely ironic.

82

"Damn and blast, who can understand you? You're a doctor, a good—"

"Stop there. One word more plunges you into error."

"But you *are* a good doctor. A fine doctor."

"A marvelous doctor. I have the deep warm voice and pretty eyes of a marvelous doctor. Universally I am thought of as marvelous. The soldier boys who have been brutalized by me, they think I am marvelous. But old Doc Jardine, he knew me for what I am, a bloody quack."

"I don't believe you."

From the inside pocket of his frock coat he withdrew a flask, tilted it, drank, and then held it toward her. She pushed it back hard. He grinned. She began shuffling papers, much too conscious of his study for anything like efficiency. While he watched he stroked the golden beard that had once been so close in color to her own hair. Now it was darker. Tarnished, he might have said, for the sake of its effect on her, had he known what she was thinking. Summer flies took over the dialogue from them until suddenly the door was thrust open and an immense black woman stood framed in it.

"Need you, ma'am."

"What's wrong, Effie?"

"We got trouble," she said and flung herself back out again, motioning for Margaret to follow.

But Peter got in front of her. "You'd best stay here," he said.

Indignantly, she pushed by him. All three, then, made their way down the corridor. He limped. Hobbled-skirted, so did she, in effect, while Effie, for all her bulk, made incredible speed. At one point Effie narrowly missed a collision with three little girls who would have been scattered like bowling pins had they not been swept out of the way by one of the orphanage nurses. Now Margaret knew how serious the matter was. No one was more tender with the children than Effie. Finally, a storage room marked Linens. There Effie waited for them before pulling open the door.

"Shut it," the man ordered and Margaret did, the last to enter.

83

Something in his posture implied drunkenness, but the revolver was held steadily enough. With it he was menacing a young black woman who stood with her back pressed against the shelves—a remarkably tall and good-looking woman. Jemima Wilson, a nurse at the orphanage. Except for the white, wide-brimmed hat she wore so often it had become her trademark, she was naked. Her clothes were in a pile before her. Not her uniform, her streetwear. Evidently she had just come in when she had been accosted. But she was not frightened. She held herself erect.

"Didn't know he had a gun," Effie said, hand to her throat.

"Ain't that the damndest hat you ever saw?" the man said, giggling.

He was in his middle forties, bald, the ridges in his naked skull cresting like the business end of a carbine shell. His faded union army uniform had once been a sergeant's, and the man himself had seen better days. He was strongly built but deteriorating. His stomach hid his belt.

"I'll take the gun, soldier," Peter said, reaching for it.

"Uh-uh. Show's not over yet. See? She's still got her hat on. Show don't end till the hat comes off."

Peter tried an unobtrusive step, and when Margaret saw how quickly the man reacted she revised her estimate of how drunk he was.

"Careful there," the man said. "I like shooting majors." Another giggle. "Either side."

"What's your name, soldier?"

"Evarts. John J. Evarts, at your service," he said, offering a mock salute.

"Soldier, you could get in serious trouble for what you're doing."

"I ain't no soldier. Shut up calling me soldier. I'm a civvy now."

"That won't keep you out of trouble."

"What trouble? For scaring *her*? She ain't no person. She's only a nigger woman. Who gets in trouble for scarin' a nigger woman?" The giggle again. "Tell you what, Major. You cooperate, and

84

maybe I'll strip her down, too, so as we can compare." A nod toward Margaret that chilled her blood.

"Be sensible," Peter said quietly. "Do you really yearn to spend a year in the lockup?"

"In a pig's arse."

"The police are already on their way," Margaret said, sensing bravado. "Major Mackenzie sent for them before we came in here."

"In a pig's arse to you, too, ma'am."

But he was not absolutely sure. He was torn. He hated to leave. Still . . . police. It had a sobering effect.

"The hat," he said, to buy time. "I ain't going no place without I see it off."

It was as if that were the cue she had been waiting for. Jemima whipped it free and threw it at him. Almost simultaneously Effie and Margaret charged forward. Effie's bulk slammed the man against the wall, knocking him down and jarring the gun from his hand. It was Peter who retrieved it. Margaret went to Jemima and helped her gather up her clothes.

"On your feet, filth," Peter said.

He obeyed with much effort, groaning lavishly in accompaniment. But as soon as he had aligned Effie between Peter and himself, he shoved her hard. And rushed for the door. When he could get free of Effie, Peter limped after him a step or two, but then gave it up.

"Everyone all right?" he asked.

General assent.

"Thank you, Dr. Mackenzie," Jemima said, calling after him as he left. "Bless you, sir."

"Bless you, Major," Effie said.

They helped Jemima finish dressing. She started to laugh. Effie grinned, too, but said, "Hush, child."

It had slight effect.

Effie slapped her.

Jemima skipped to the far corner of the room, out of reach. "That Dr. Mackenzie," she said, "he sure enough desperate to

85

mind his manners." Her glance flicked to Margaret. "I mean he sure enough trying hard not to look. Why he do that, Mrs. Jardine? He a doctor, ain't he? What's so special about a naked woman to a doctor?"

Effie said, "Pay her no mind, Mrs. Jardine. She half hysterical. She forget how a nurse supposed to act. Best let her just run down."

"That Doctor Mackenzie, he in a botheration to remember how a doctor supposed to act."

"Jemima," Margaret said warningly.

"Jemima," Effie said, "you better quit now. Else I'm going to catch you up and rattle you till your ears fall off."

Eyes dancing wickedly, Jemima edged toward the door. "I think he itching for that comparison."

The door slammed behind her.

In a mirror nailed to one of the shelves Margaret examined deeply red cheeks. She kept her back to Effie until the color faded.

When she returned to her office she found Peter at her desk, feet slung on top of it. "She ain't no person. She's only a nigger woman," he said, echoing the erstwhile sergeant. "I'll tell you a story, Margaret, would you like that?"

She kept silent.

"Well, I'll tell it to you anyway. Last winter it was. We had just taken another in our series of beatings from Johnny Reb, and we were camped out near Fredericksburg, licking our wounds. Fifth corps, seventh regiment, Army of the Potomac, General S. L. Macklin, commanding. You know General Macklin, long-time admirer of your father's. Let's see now—winter, I said. Must have been middle December because I had two feet then, I remember, and I looked up from trying to clean the mud off one of them to see—what? You're not going to ask? No matter. To see Colonel J. R. Bunce, second to General Macklin, commanding, as he gives the order to tear down for firewood two ramshackle wooden sheds—in which a dozen or so blacks had been taking shelter. Did I mention that among these there were a fair sprinkling of babies and elderly folk? Well, there were. At any rate when I remon-

86

strated with said Colonel Bunce, saying that no person of conscience would treat people that way, I remember how he gazed at me. Blank-faced at first and then as if I had taken leave of my senses. 'But they are niggers, sir,' he said, as if somehow my eyes had been closed to this. 'And General Macklin is cold and wet.'"

Margaret found she had to hug herself to repress a shudder.

He tipped back the flask.

Without pausing to consider, she sprang forward, reaching for it. She had not really known she was going to do that, but there the flask was in her hand. She raced to the window. He had a shorter distance to travel and could cut her off. With the ferocity of enraged animals they battled wordlessly, she to get a throwing arm free; he to prevent her. And then suddenly the battle ended. Or if it did not, it became a battle of another sort since his mouth was savaging hers, and his surgeon-powerful hands were gripping her in a way that should have been painful. But she felt only his mouth. Until he shoved her away.

"Oh, God," he said.

His breathing, she decided, made the same sharp ugly sound hers did. She felt so strange, as if the inside of her head were thick heavy cotton. One could not think through that much cotton.

"Damn you, I counted on you," he said.

Her glance was nailed to the floor. She knew she could not lift it without tearing something vital. She tried to speak. Nothing came out. To her horror she started to cry.

"Oh, for God's sake," he said, but his voice was gentler.

She could not stop. And she was almost more ashamed of that than anything else. "I've been a good wife to Stephen," she said. And wanted to die. The words had nothing to do with what she had really planned to say. Except she could not concentrate on whatever that was.

"I know."

"What did you mean—counted on me?"

"To keep us from giving in. Everybody knows I have no character. You were supposed to have enough for both."

87

"Are you suggesting that I . . ." She broke off. She took a shuddery breath and started for the door.

"Where are you going?"

"Home."

"Damn it, sit. You can't leave this office looking like that. Effie will think I've been beating you."

She sat. There was silence again. She could not bear the way it was accumulating. "Why did you come back?" she said. "You promised you never would."

"I had no choice. They sent me back."

Some weight bent her head. Her gaze returned to the floor, remained fixed there as if in its shiny surface she could see fateful things.

"What happened just now . . ." She stopped and started over again. "You were quite right, of course. For what happened just now I bear a share of the responsibility. But it must never be repeated."

"Must never be repeated," he said mockingly. He took the flask from the table, pocketed it, and limped from the room.

3

A few minutes past nine, and though Broadway was beginning to show Sunday sleepiness, it was not quite ready to be put to bed. At Forty-second Street a half-filled omnibus closed in on its final run, but store windows for the most part remained brightly lighted as were the entrances of all the hotels. Strollers were very much in evidence; sidewalk musicians, too, still playing to typical Sunday audiences, which is to say larger since the Sunday shutters were up on the theatres. And then, of course:

"How do you do, my dear? There's a good time to be had if you come home with me."

With their scarlet shawls, bare shoulders, and bogus diamonds flashing in the moonlight.

"Begone with you," Brautigan said. "Unless you want my stick on your hind quarters."

"Whoosht, I'm that scairt."

But when he stepped toward her, off she skedaddled. Brautigan turned to Stephen. "What was she, fourteen?"

Stephen stopped abruptly and made his friend do the same. Brautigan was not in uniform, and Stephen's glance swept appreciatively over the well-cut beige frock coat and dark brown cravat; noted the snowy linen; took stock of the boutonniere.

"The clothes are lively enough," he said, "but the mood is black Irish. Let me guess: Rosie."

Deepening scowl.

"Bad as that?"

"It's over. Nor do I wish to talk about it."

He shook off Stephen's hand and resumed his pace. Stephen caught up to him. And then, seemingly apropos of nothing, said, "Do you remember the day we filched a flagon of the housemaster's brandy and made off with it to St. John's Park? We sat behind the dunes talking about life."

"And getting drunker by the minute," Brautigan said, the trace of a smile despite himself.

"And sicker by the minute."

"Yes."

"Babes," Stephen said.

"Sixteen, I think. I remember you said you had decided not to marry. Women were a plague and a botheration, as I recall. They seldom understood a fellow. They liked the wrong things about a fellow. And often they came between good fellows."

"I was hard on women that day," Stephen said.

"No more than their due," Brautigan said, sour again. But this time he stopped. "Ah, hell, Stephen, it's never her fault. It's all mine, every bit of it. I began something I should not have."

And Stephen needed another burst of speed to catch up.

By the time he did, they had arrived at the bronze door of the St. Nicholas Hotel. "You asked her to marry you, and she said no? Is that it?"

Brautigan kept silent.

"Of course not," Stephen said in reply to himself. "*You* said no. What a fool you are, John Brautigan. Go see Tyrell. You will find me waiting to talk sense to you when your meeting is over."

"No reason to."

"Damn you, I said I would wait."

90

Brautigan, having witnessed a flash of temper long familiar to him, turned without further argument.

He climbed the broad staircase. The St. Nicholas was new—and in its sumptuousness the talk of the city—but when he paused on the landing it was not to admire the two-hundred-foot sweep of the magnificent hall. Nor the chandeliers and wall sconces by the dozens; nor the effect of gaslight gleaming brilliantly in the mirrors that ran throughout. Tonight Brautigan was impervious to the impact of interior design. He had stopped on the landing solely to gird his loins; to force himself to contend with the business at hand. Hatred awaited him: Tyrell.

Like all good police officers, Brautigan was no stranger to hatred. You put on the uniform and there it was. You met it daily if you did the job you were expected to. But Tyrell's hatred went far enough beyond the ordinary that Brautigan would have given it a name of its own if he could have thought of one. And it was inexplicable, Tyrell's hatred; that is, there was no cause and effect to it; no place on the map that could be isolated and identified as its source of origin. Spontaneous combustion is what it was. Something about Brautigan was so inimical to Tyrell that the course of their relationship had never been in doubt, set immutably on the day of that initial Chrystie Street confrontation.

Not that it had been all that much of a confrontation. A small thing in its line to be so life-altering. A ball had come bouncing toward him as he emerged from his building. He had retrieved it and had been about to return it to the boys clustered some twenty yards up the block, five or six of them. One of them called out, "To me," and he had been about to obey when the voice called out again, "Come on, come on, throw the bloody ball here." Something in the tone, some high degree of peremptoriness, had caused Brautigan to pause and then make a point of tossing the ball to one of the other boys. Nothing more. He had continued on his way—to Kerrigan's Grocery-Groggery on an errand for his mother—without further incident. Except, of course, for the exchange of stares as he passed Tyrell. These had fixed their fates.

He heard his name called. A small dapper man in evening

clothes was hurrying toward him, Supervisor Benton. Bald, in his late sixties, but with snapping blue eyes. He smoked a large black cigar and swung his cane in hectic but authoritative flurries.

"Saw Jardine downstairs," Benton said, breathing just a touch rapidly while he pretended this was not the case. "Told him he could join us if he would keep it off the record, but he said Greeley gave express orders against."

"I know." Brautigan, with tact, gave his attention to an opulently framed seascape. Soon the supervisor's chest recovered its normal rise and fall.

"Greeley must have threatened to shoot Jardine," he said. "Either that, or he didn't much want to come up here anyway. Because God knows he ain't that easily headed. Like you, come to think of it."

"Worse."

"Well, move along, move along. And keep in mind the mayor's sensibilities. I mean if you can't behave like a decent Republican, at least don't act like a bloody Democrat."

Brautigan grunted. "Tyrell wouldn't let me if I wanted to."

Benton led the way into the "Gentleman's Parlor," a huge room with heavy damask curtains and an immense oak table. Around this were seated five men, all of whom would have been instantly recognizable to Stephen Jardine, or any other reasonably alert New York newspaperman. There were the mayor, Albert Gibbons; General Macklin of New York's own Seventh Regiment, and Colonel Bunce, his aide. These were on the Republican side of the table. Facing them were the Democrats: Boss Tyrell and Police Commissioner Robbo Royce. The room was silent. All five held coffee cups into which they stared as intently as if their fortunes were in the grinds. Only Tyrell looked up as Benton and Brautigan entered. But as he did, everything in his face awoke. Brautigan appreciated the irony: hates me, yes, but I have never bored him.

Tyrell said, "Hail, the minions of the law."

Brautigan nodded at Royce who ceased wiping his brow long enough to nod in return.

What there was of air was heavy with cigar smoke. At the far

92

end of the room was another table, smaller, on which was a stupendous silver coffee urn. Next to that was a large tray of generously made sandwiches. (The remains of at least two of these were on a plate before Tyrell. No one else seemed to have partaken.) Next to the tray was a portable bar, stocked to the limits of its measurements. And next to that, ready to dispense on command, was a thin old black man. He had very white hair and very empty, straight-ahead eyes. It was as if he did not exist except for dispensing purposes.

Brautigan knew him. His name was Frederick Berryman, and Brautigan had once arrested him for assault. A fight with a white man over ownership of a dray horse. Rightfully Berryman's, the judge had decided, but three months hard labor (down from six) for Berryman nonetheless, coinciding with the period required for his adversary to recover from a series of knife wounds. A long time ago. If Berryman remembered Brautigan he made no sign.

Mayor Gibbons indicated the spread. "Whatever your pleasure, gentlemen."

Both declined.

Royce, grinning, said, "Abstemious minions of the law."

Tyrell said, "Just whilst anyone's looking."

General Macklin stood. Undersized and only months from seventy and retirement, he was still an imposing presence. He had a tyrant's charisma. Bald head, heavy white mustache, colorless eyes. He tapped Bunce's shoulder. Bunce, florid, fat-cheeked, the armpits of his khaki uniform ringed with sweat, rose instantly. He said, "General Macklin is a busy man. He is responsible for the safety of this entire city. The entire city, Tyrell—including your filthy wards. He has no time for tomfoolery."

Tyrell raised a choirboy's glance. "What did I do now?"

"The general objects to your tone."

"My tone is it? Oh, well now the supervisor ain't what you'd call a sensitive man. And as for the chief inspector . . . we go back aways, don't we, John?"

Brautigan smiled humorlessly.

"The general—"

"Thank God for the general and his watchin' over us, that's what I always say. Tell him, Robbo. Ain't that what I always say?"

"On his knees," Royce said. "Nightly. For without him who could sleep peaceful in this wicked city?"

Mayor Gibbons hit the table with a heavy fist. "Enough," he said. But then, having taken the breath experienced politicians learn to take, he said, "Your forbearance, General Macklin."

The general hesitated. Not a perspicacious man, he knew nevertheless that he had been insulted. Flagrantly? The issue hung in the balance until, through body language incomprehensible to the rest, he sent a signal to Bunce. Both resumed their seats. So did Tyrell, grinning. Gibbons glared at him.

Gibbons and Tyrell were big men. Big shoulders, big chests. Stomachs shaped by good living. In a sense a matched pair, Brautigan thought, though neither would have enjoyed the bracketing.

Gibbons turned to Benton. Taking the cue, Benton reached into his pocket for a carefully folded piece of paper and examined its contents, but then instead of reading from it, he refolded it and said, "I believe there is dangerous unrest."

"Humbug," Tyrell said.

"I believe General Macklin should alert the seventh and hold it in readiness."

"Martial law, too?" Tyrell demanded. And then whirled to face Gibbons. "You better bloody not. You can't declare martial law without Governor Spencer's say so."

"Do you know where the governor is?"

"Don't you?"

"I have sent six wires to Albany. And since I have not been favored with a reply, I am doing him the courtesy of assuming he is not there. Am I wrong?"

Tyrell finished his sandwich with a carnivorous flourish.

"I think he ought to be sent for," Gibbons said. "If you know where he is—"

Lifting the flap of his weskit pocket, Tyrell pretended to peer inside.

94

Gibbons flamed up. "It's the governor of the state of New York I have reference to. Not Royce or some other graft-hungry politician."

"Saints alive," Royce said mildly, "the rough side of his honor's tongue."

Benton unfolded the paper again. "Dispatch to Chief Inspector John Brautigan," he read. "A man named Campfield . . . no first name ascertainable . . . has been holding meetings of an incendiary nature at several salients in the sixth and seventh wards. Unrest seems to be increasing. Officer Dempsey estimates crowd of one thousand at Twenty-third and Second Avenue. Some informants say Campfield is a Virginian, others a Kentuckian. One usually reliable informant insists he is a Confederate operative, who has been here often before on clandestine missions. Dempsey and O'Malley attempted to detain said Campfield but were forestalled by mob. Threats and obscenities. Officers forced to flee. Do not at all like the mood of the populace. Await instructions as to Campfield. He has gone underground somewhere. Should we search? Signed Daniel J. O'Hara, Captain."

"Oh, for God's sake," Tyrell said. "Just a few Sunday beers and letting off steam. No more to it than that. That's the trouble with you aristocrats. You have no feel for the people. A loud voice here and there scares the bejesus out of you. Let's go, Robbo."

They were almost at the door when Brautigan spoke, calling Tyrell by his first name.

Tyrell stopped as if roped.

"In the sixth ward they are talking about decorating lamp posts with black men," Brautigan said.

Tyrell looked at Berryman, who remained statuelike. "With niggers you mean," he said.

"And the talk is spreading."

"They don't like the draft. And they don't like niggers. Say something that matters."

"How's this, Terence? If they start burning houses you own fifty to my one."

Tyrell came back into the room. "If they start burning houses they won't be Tyrell's," he said.

Their glances held. Royce pulled gently at Tyrell's sleeve, did so again before Tyrell nodded, as if to himself, as if in confirmation of some privately held theory and turned to leave, Royce in his wake. But when he reached Berryman he stopped once more. He said, "You a freedman, nigger?"

"Yes, sir."

Tyrell snapped his fingers. "Give him something, Robbo. Give him ten dollars. Here, nigger. Find yourself some room on a packet boat. Go back to Africa where President Linkum says you'll be happy."

Berryman took the money. "Thank you, sir."

Tyrell to Brautigan, grinning. "Who says I ain't a friend to the nigger?"

Brautigan kept silent.

Tyrell's grin widened. "A friend to the nigger, and the deservin' poor. Young Michael sends his regards, John. Like one of them picture postcards, see. On the front of it, there's this scene, the view from the top of Tammany Hall. So beautiful . . . lots of the green stuff. And I ain't talking about grass or trees, am I? And on the back Michael writes, 'Havin' a wonderful time, Pop.'"

Brautigan kept silent.

Tyrell watched him. After a moment he said, mildly: "Look both ways when you cross a street, John."

He left, Royce hurrying to keep pace.

A silence, heavy and dispiriting. Then Gibbons said, "Were I you, Chief Inspector, I would not take the advice casually."

"No, sir. I don't."

"What an appalling man."

"Right about the niggers though," General Macklin said. "Happier in Africa."

"You may leave us, Berryman," Gibbons said and waited for his exit.

"Uppity nigger," Macklin said. "You can tell by the way he moves. You can always tell if you know your niggers."

96

To Benton, Gibbons said, "Aside from that bred in the bone nastiness, what game is Tyrell playing?"

Benton shrugged. "Politics . . . Tammany-style . . . at the outset, is my guess. Manufacture a bit of a muss and count on people remembering come election day. And remembering that all the bother happened under a Republican administration. At least that's how it started. But now I think he may be sweating a little, worrying it could bust loose."

"Suppose it does? What then? Does he ally himself with us?"

"He'll have to, won't he? What choice does he have? John's right. He owns more New York real estate than the Astors."

Gibbons fished his watch from his pocket and stared at it— unseeingly, Brautigan knew, having recognized the look of a man seeking comfort from habit while struggling with a decision. Finally, turning to General Macklin, he said, "I know it's a bore, but let us be safe. Perhaps an alert to two companies of the seventh, have them on standby."

Dismissed a few minutes later, Brautigan found Berryman waiting for him.

Opening his palm, Berryman let a shredded ten dollar bill flutter to the floor. "I'm fixing to kill that man," he said.

Brautigan started to push by him.

"You don't believe me?"

"If you kill him I'll find you and put you in jail. That's all the concern it is of mine. Stay out of trouble, Berryman. My jail's no nicer today than it ever was."

Berryman grinned. It was like seeing a death mask come to life. "How many times you done tell me to stay out of trouble?"

"Seems like a lot."

"I remember one time though."

"Stuff that. I helped you then because I thought they gave you a skinning. And the truth is, old man, you've passed your time for killing."

"That the truth, sure enough?"

He reached into his white jacket and from a sheath fastened under his arm withdrew a long thin Italianate knife with a brass

97

snake as it's handle. Brautigan had seen it once before, imbedded in the left bicep of the man who had attempted to commandeer Berryman's horse. "Appears like you're right. Look at ol' Bess here, shivering in this poor ol' hand. Nothing but the weakness left in this poor ol' darky." His eyes gleamed with uncut wickedness, but then the light went out. Or was put out. Brautigan found it impossible to tell. He watched the old man shamble from view and then went downstairs to collect Stephen.

4

From Stephen Jardine's diary. Sunday, July 2:

Restless and headachy. Could not write. Could not even sit still. The god-awful heat. That plus the flickering of a faulty candle. Elected to take my aching head outdoors. Encountered a Broadway omnibus going north, and, on impulse, boarded it. Thought for a while of riding it out to One hundred thirty-seventh, the last street in the city, but knew I would have trouble finding an omnibus coming back. And did not want to be stranded with the cows, chickens, farmers, etc. Got off at Sixtieth, which has fewer cows & Co. Greeley insists the city's northward march has barely begun. Forecasts a population of three million souls a century hence and wonders why I will not take him seriously.

What a city it is *now*. A city stretching for greatness. But also a city of ugliness and corruption. A city in which public monies are shamefully wasted (and stolen) by political rakehells such as Terence Tyrell. A city whose streets are illpaved and broken by carts and omnibuses into ruts and dangerous gullies. A city never adequately cleaned. A city in which the traffic chokes the thoroughfares; in which virtually all drivers of all vehicles dash recklessly about, heedless of the women and children struggling to survive them. A city in which rowdyism rules; in which it takes lion-hearts or fools to walk the streets at night, since the pistol, the knife, the slingshot, and the garrote are in such constant activity. 'Tis a city of which one frequently despairs. And never tires. And, according to Greeley, 'tis yet but a babe of a city.

And, if this city takes seriously the alarums about civil strife, it hides its concern well.

By half past nine I was back at Thirtieth Street and had much peripatetic company. Belles and dandies parading in the summer night as if only Martians faced the draft. Consider Beresford, ill met at the corner of Fourth Avenue and Twenty-third. One more block and I would have been safely home. Luxuriant mustaches, brilliantined curls, gleaming patent leather shoes. And, despite the heat, white kid gloves. He was in my class at Columbia, and a silly ass even then.

Draft? What draft? War? What war? My dear chap—and flicks my shoulder with his delicate kids—you must know the Beresfords never go to war. Tee-hee. And there I stand for a good quarter hour, enduring him. Short-tempered, they call me. Saintly, more like it—and Beresford the living proof.

Young Stephen takes precautionary leave of us by first ferry tomorrow, a visit to his Aunt Singleton—Rosie in attendance. Margaret's sensible idea.

It would be equally sensible for her to go as well. And if I should ever encounter her again I will most certainly suggest it.

Monday
July
3,
1863

Though only a few minutes past eight, there was no longer any doubt about the kind of day it was going to be. A scorcher. And as Cora rushed to make up the time she had lost by dawdling, she knew, helplessly, that streamlets of sweat were already discoloring the back of her dress. Where had the morning gone? Nathaniel's breakfast . . . a bit of dusting . . . a bit of laundry . . . a pair of socks that needed darning . . . and irrevocably she was behind schedule. Due at the orphanage by nine, she was never going to make it. Effie would be understanding. Jemima would be all over her with teasing. Both would be difficult to take, since no one spoke with more disdain of tardiness than Cora herself. She sighed in annoyance. She liked to think of herself as the kind of person who invariably did what was expected of her; as responsible, a bulwark. Not the kind who could be sidetracked by reveries, daydreams, and such.

Finally, bonnet tied, shawl in place, she was ready to unlock the front door when she heard a furious banging against it. And then Willie Jones's voice, high-pitched and excited: "Reverend Dawson. For the lord's sake, open up."

When he saw it was Cora he automatically lowered his voice, but there was no lessening of intensity. "Let us in, Sister Cora. Please. We have to hide."

With him was Lieutenant Frazier whose forehead was bleeding from a jagged cut, his uniform ripped at the shoulder, but whose irritating smile was intact.

Cora stepped away from the door so they could get by, and then led them into her bedroom. Shutting that door, too, she asked, "Who is after you?" In the one brief glimpse she had allowed herself she had seen only empty street.

"White trash, that's who," Willie said. "Whole mob of them. They wants to hurt us bad."

"But why?"

"The uniform," Frazier said.

"I don't understand."

"It maddens them."

"That's right, Sister Cora," Willie said. "The sight of that uniform done drove that white trash crazy. My, oh, my, oh, my." He looked at Frazier and suddenly he was grinning. In the next moment Frazier was, too. And then they were hugging each other, laughing, unable to stop.

Cora was appalled. "Enough! Have you both lost your minds?"

"You should have seen them," Willie said, gasping. "They was having cat fits. They were frothing at the mouth. They was having conniptions. Like he done took a paint brush into their church. That's right. That's what it was. That blue uniform on that black body was like black paint on Jesus' white face."

"A desecration," Frazier said.

She turned and started out of the room.

"Sister Cora," Frazier said sharply.

She stopped.

But then for the first time since she had met him he seemed uncertain. "If we're unwelcome . . ."

"When you are, Lieutenant, I'll be happy to let you know. In the meantime I'm going to get something to put on that cut."

She shut the door behind her and leaned against it for a

104

moment. Safe from inspection, she yielded to the shivery weakness she had felt growing in her. What was it? How explain the
effect that man had on her? Good-looking? Yes, he was certainly
that, with that special color to his skin her cousin Deborah called
mulatto maize. And the high-bridged nose, bold chin, moody
eyes, strong, slim-hipped body. You could see the African warrior
and the plantation aristocrat incessantly choosing sides over
him—a tilt toward the former when he was being fierce; toward
the latter when his eyes went sleepy and he chose to charm. All of
this was interesting enough. Still, she had known good-looking
men before, and, yes, several of them had tried to get round her.
Dull, vain peacocks, by and large. No trouble fending them off. But
this one . . . this Frazier . . .

She caught her breath, shut her eyes, waited for the spasm to
pass. Angrily, then, she pushed away from the door. A few
seconds later she was in full control of herself and briskly going
about the business of filling a pan with hot water and tearing the
bottom from an old petticoat for use as a bandage.

"Where's the reverend?" Willie asked when she returned.

"Deacons' meeting," she said.

"At the church?" Frazier asked.

"Yes."

"You thinking of hiding out there?" Willie asked.

"For a while." Frazier looked at Cora. "That is if Reverend
Dawson will let us."

"Oh, he'll let you, all right," Cora said. "He'll welcome you with
open arms." By this time she had set the bowl down on the table,
seated him on the bed next to her, and was dabbing at the cut,
which when cleansed appeared insignificant. "He enjoys these
small boy's games almost as much as you do."

Willie put his foot down. "He ain't going nowhere, Sister Cora,
until I runs to my house and gets him something to wear instead
of that uniform. That blue uniform like a red flag," he said and
grinned at the accidental joke. A moment later he was gone.

Having locked and bolted the door behind him, Cora returned to

105

Frazier. She finished treating his cut. She realized, suddenly, that he was grinning at her.

"How glad I am to be able to amuse you," she said.

He reached for her hand. "Now, now, Sister Cora, don't go upsetting yourself. It's not just you I'm giggling at. It's us. Time to declare a truce."

Slowly, inexorably, he raised her hand to his mouth, so slowly that by the time it got there her heart seemed to have expanded to fill not only her chest cavity but the area usually reserved for her stomach. His eyes never left hers. Shockingly, he kissed the back of her hand, a knuckle at a time. Then he turned her hand around and kissed the pads beneath each of her fingers and finally the center of her palm. She made no attempt whatsoever to pull her hand away. She was paralyzed. As were her vocal chords. She couldn't speak. Breathing was painful.

He let her hand drop.

She shuddered.

"Sure looks like we want each other," he said.

"If by want you mean—"

"Hush."

He placed his hands at the sides of her head so that they formed a vise. His forehead touched hers. The thought that he was about to kiss her mouth so occupied her that all other activity became peripheral. At that moment she could not have said if she wanted the kiss or didn't. But the idea of it was overwhelming.

He did not kiss her. Instead his hands slipped to her shoulders, and he shook her a little. "Confess," he said. "You'll feel better for it."

"I do not enjoy being mocked," she said.

"You don't know yet what you enjoy."

And before she could reply his mouth lowered to hers, landing with little force and even less duration.

But she yearned to be enraged. One part of her craved the words with which to whip him mercilessly—words like seducer, corrupter, blackguard, cad, villain. She knew they existed, but she couldn't find them.

106

She managed to say, "That was hateful of you."

"Yes," he said and kissed her again.

It seemed to her she fainted.

She groaned, and when she could, said, "What are you doing to me?"

"It's called making love," he said without interrupting the devastating work his hands were involved in.

"But it's wicked."

"Do you want me to stop?" he asked. "If you want me to, I will."

She felt that this was smugness in him, and it sparked a last vestige of fury. "Doesn't it bother you that I am a respectable woman? That you are a guest in my brother's house?"

"No."

"That you're a preacher's son?"

"I was a preacher's son. In some other life."

"What are you now?"

"A man growing old so quickly it amazes me."

But then he moved away from her. "There's the door. On your way now, little Cora. Lock it one side or the other."

He gave her a mild shove. At first she thought she might have a chance to make it through. Her beginning steps were brisk. Halfway there she stopped. She looked back at her. Resolve crumpled. It was an old woman, then, who turned the key in the lock and slumped against the door.

"Apparently you can make me do whatever you wish," she said. "I hope you're satisfied."

He said nothing. He came to her, swinging her up in his arms and carried her to her bed. She shut her eyes. He began to undress her. She lay corpselike. If the capacity for movement still existed it was minimal, she thought. He didn't seem to mind. And then, like a betrayal, stiffness fled her body. She felt boneless. She felt as if she might suffocate. She felt as if she might scream. And she felt frightened.

Now she was naked, and his hands left her. A moment passed, and she knew he was naked, too.

107

He got in bed next to her. He stroked her—her neck, her back, her shoulders. She began to relax.

"You're perfect, little Cora," he said.

She could actually laugh.

"You like that?"

"It's odd to think of oneself as perfect."

"Well, you are."

"And you?"

"Open your eyes and see."

"Never."

His mouth on hers, not gentle now, his tongue forcing its way past her teeth, stalking hers. Hands on her breasts, fingers racing, probing deeply into that dread, drenched place she had known all along was a destination. She tried to buck him out of there. But he stayed. He made inroads. And now she knew her body had changed masters, that all the turning and twisting was in his behalf.

"Open your eyes, Cora," he said. Peremptory.

She did. She had no choice. She was without will. And he was over her—taut, menacing.

She mumbled something.

"What?" he asked.

"Unfair."

"Have you had many women?"

He laughed.

Piqued, she said, "Why should that amuse you, Lieutenant?"

"I think you might call me Richard."

"I want to know why that was funny."

"*Richard.*"

"Very well—Richard."

"Because women have been asking it of their men for centuries."

"Have they? Well, you see I know so little of all that. I've been debauched for only an hour or so."

He turned so that he could study her. "Debauched. Is that how you feel?"

She was unable to meet his eyes. "No," she said, burrowing into him. "I no doubt should, but I don't. I feel . . . cherished."

He kissed the tip of her nose. "Thank you."

"But have there been many women? My brother told me you spent two years in Paris. Is that where most of your women were?"

"Only the first hundred."

She pinched him cruelly.

"My God, Cora."

Following an extra tweak for good measure, she released him. She touched his hair. It was stiff, tightly coiled. She took a tendril of it to her lips. After a moment she said, "When you leave I will follow. You will hate me for that, I know, but I can't help myself. You have made me shameless."

He started to smile, then stopped; froze. An instant later he was off the bed and across the room. Carefully, he pushed the curtain aside and peered through the window.

"What is it?" Cora asked.

He motioned her to silence.

All at once she felt quite cold. She gathered the blankets around her and backed up against the headboard. She watched him. He was all soldier now. Tense, alert. Gone the smiling, indolent lover.

"I heard something out there," he said.

"What?"

"Voices."

"But there are always voices in the street."

He shook his head impatiently. "As if orders were being given. And I do believe, little Cora, that someone is watching the house." He turned toward her. "We'd best settle for what we can from your brother's wardrobe."

"Richard—"

"Do the best you can. Whatever it is will be better than the uniform. Hurry."

She did. When she returned with the clothes he was still kneeling at the window. His back was toward her. He looked like a piece of ebony sculpture. Except that he was shiny with sweat. She knelt next to him. She touched his neck.

109

He smiled. His eyes, however, remained fixed on a squat, red-roofed shack across the street. Old Nicey Trumbull lived there, a runaway slave from Beaufort, South Carolina. He had turned up two years ago and charmed everyone in the neighborhood with the irrepressible delight he took in being free. Lame, in his seventies, he was an indefatigable fiddler. Almost always he could be seen on his front porch, on his ancient rocker, fiddle in hand—sometimes making music, sometimes just available for passing the time of day. But now the rocker was empty. For some reason this shot a thrill of fear through Cora.

"All I could find," she said and handed him the black broadcloth jacket, torn at the sleeve, and the brown broadcloth pantaloons, torn at the seat—garments made for a man fifty pounds heavier than Richard Frazier.

A swift grin passed over his face, but then it was gone. Both dressed hurriedly. While they did she told him about Nicey, hoping he would make light of her fear.

"Silly to be upset by that, Richard, I know it is. Except he's always there. I mean even when it rains he just pushes the rocker back under the eaves a little."

He saw her bite her lip, and in response took her in his arms. "Nothing to worry about, ma'am. This here's Lieutenant Frazier looking after you now. Nothing to worry about from now on."

At that moment the quiet in the street ended abruptly. They heard loud voices, the sound of feet running toward them—from Nicey's house: two white men, now only a dozen yards away, both shouting, one voice louder than the other.

"We know you're in there, niggers."

Cora hadn't even seen the pistol until Frazier broke the window with it. An instant later she heard the shot, and the frontrunner, the larger of the two, the one with the black knit cap and bright red pantaloons, went down. The other stopped at once. By this time he was no more than two yards away. He stared at her. He looked down at his friend. He was a boy—seventeen, eighteen at the most. Cora thought she recognized him, one of the drivers for the milk company. A sob burst from him. He turned and ran.

110

The fallen man—much older, in his forties perhaps—groaned. Automatically, Cora started to go to him but was pulled back.

"I'm a nurse," she said. "He may be dying."

"I hope so," he said.

She looked at him. His face was expressionless—no hate there, nothing at all but absolute alertness. His fingers tightened on her wrist, hurting her.

"Let's go," he said.

2

Clearly, it was not your workaday Monday morning at 200 Mulberry Street, Stephen decided the moment he pushed through the heavy front door of the converted armory that was now metropolitan police headquarters. For one thing he had never seen Robbo Royce there that early (half past eight), nor that many people in general, civilians as well as police. All of them looked anxious.

A crowd of fifty or so was collected in the large anteroom outside Supervisor Benton's office. They more or less formed a circle. In the approximate center of this were two of John Brautigan's sergeants: Tim Prendergast and Kevin O'Neill. On the perimeter Stephen recognized reporters and politicos, a handful of the city's leading merchants, as well as a handful of the city's better known busybodies.

The sergeants were excited. Big Prendergast, face florid, mopped at his brow, pried his collar free of his suffering jowls. "Couple of hundred of them at least," he said. "With crowbars, clubs—"

"Bailing hooks," said O'Neill. "Whatever they could get their hands on."

"That's right," Prendergast said. "Whatever. And carrying their signs."

"No Bloody Draft."

"Women, too."

"Women, too," O'Neill echoed. "I mean women was all over the piers everywhere you looked. And everywhere you looked there were them No Bloody Draft signs, all sizes, hand-lettered."

"Some was printed," Prendergast said.

"I didn't see any was printed."

Supervisor Benton smacked his cane on the table, from behind which he and Royce were interrogating the policemen. Oddly enough it had a calming effect.

"I don't much care if the signs were hand-printed or lettered in gold," he said. "I would like to know where you think the mob was heading."

The larger man deferred to the smaller. "Central Park, sir," O'Neill said.

Royce, jovial for the benefit of the reporters: "Central Park? Now that ain't much of a threat to anything."

"Sir," O'Neill said, "A lot of them are boozed up pretty good."

"At this hour of the morning?" Benton was startled despite himself.

"They've been busting into saloons and grog shops all along Broadway. I mean *all* the shops. I mean every one they come to."

A stir from the onlookers.

"I told you that, Royce," a deep voice said angrily.

In a full-bearded age, Jacob Astor was clean-shaven. A large man in his middle years, he once, certainly, had been physically impressive. Now, however, he was given over to roundness. This offered the appearance of jollity. Deceptive. Stephen, who had known him first as a poker-playing crony of his father's, was not surprised to see how respectfully heads swiveled in Astor's direction. He had about him that aura of power, rooted in his

113

owning more unimproved Fifth Avenue square footage than any other real estate speculator in New York.

"I told you that in no uncertain terms," Astor said, "and expected you to . . . relay the information."

"I did," Royce said unhappily.

"Well?"

Royce wet his lips and said nothing.

The unspoken name was Tyrell's of course, and everyone waited to see if Astor was in a mood for confrontation. For a moment it seemed he might be. And to Stephen the special sound of journalistic breaths drawn in was easily audible. But then Astor turned away. Actually it was an all but simultaneous turning—an unpremeditated duet—Astor in disgust; Royce in relief.

The hubbub broke out anew. From the *Herald*'s Kirby: "What I want to know is who are the leaders? Is that man Campfield among them?"

Prendergast had his mouth open to answer when Benton's stick hit the table again. "Enough!" he said. "This is not a damn press conference. You will please keep in mind, gentlemen, that you are here on sufferance."

Stephen thought it was time Benton got pushed a little. He was trying to have it all his own way. And when the police had it all their own way, that meant muzzling was just around the corner.

"You asked us here, and now you want us playing dead," he said.

"I did not ask you here. The mayor gave his permission for you to be here."

From the *Tribune*'s Morrison: "Where *is* the mayor?"

From Kirby: "Where's the governor?"

Benton's outraged voice transcending: "Damn it, enough!"

The reporters looked at Stephen. Stephen looked at the ceiling. He saw a crack there that could bring to mind the Mississippi wending its way south to just above Vicksburg. Eyes narrowed, mouth puckered in a silent whistle, he mapped its progress. When he decided he'd been at cartography long enough to make his point, he grinned—his signal to the press corps that he was backing off. As usual the corps picked up its cue.

"Thank you," Benton said, his glance at Stephen not ungrateful. "The governor is on his way from his vacation cottage in Monmouth. Mayor Gibbons is in his office awaiting him. The mayor has asked me to tell you they will probably issue a joint statement around noon. Is that satisfactory for now?"

Decorous murmurs of assent.

Benton returned his attention to the sergeants. "*Was* Campfield anywhere to be seen?"

Prendergast looked at O'Neill, who said, "He was supposed to have been at Pier Seven."

"Supposed to have been?"

"We never set eyes on him, but one of Prendy's informants gave a description that was a pretty good fit."

"Recognize anyone else?"

"You mean known troublemakers, sir?"

"If that's what I mean, did you?"

"No, sir."

"Explain."

Now O'Neill looked at Prendergast.

Benton punished the desk. "Come on, come on, men; let's have it."

"Lots of me friends and neighbors," O'Neill said grimly.

There was a moment of silence as everyone considered the implications of this. The front door was opened again, and Brautigan entered. Unhurriedly he made his way through the crowd—it parted readily for him—to Benton's desk.

"May I see you in your office, supervisor?"

Stephen said, "Hell with that, John. We know we're dealing with a tinderbox. That's why Gibbons has us down here, because he wants the newspapers backing him. Well, if that's the way he wants it, no closed doors."

Brautigan waited for a signal from Benton. The supervisor shrugged, then nodded. Brautigan said, "They're dragging people out of the shops and factories left and right. Not that most of them

115

have to be dragged if you want the God's honest truth. I just crossed Seventh and Eighth avenues, and they're both jammed with horsecars. Bumper to bumper. No drivers in a one of them. That's because the drivers are marching, too."

At a signal from Stephen, Morrison cut for the door—half a dozen colleagues after him.

Several of the other reporters wanted it verified that the mob's destination remained Central Park. Brautigan assured them that was being loudly proclaimed, and they scrambled out in the *Tribune* man's wake. Benton detached two squads of police. He told them, firmly, they were on reconnoitering duty, instructing them to avoid any kind of contact with the mob that could be possibly construed as inflammatory. Shortly thereafter the exodus became general as the politicians and the merchants left on errands that had to do with the shoring up of their own defences. And the busybodies followed their noses to Central Park. Except for Stephen and Jacob Astor, now the building contained only police.

Brautigan said, "Central Park first but then the provost marshal's."

Astor nodded and Benton said, "They'll tear the place apart."

Brautigan turned to Stephen. "Coming down here, did you by chance pass the provost marshal's?"

"Still quiet," Stephen said.

To Benton, Brautigan said, "Between the Sixth and Eighteenth precincts we can probably muster sixty men and get them to Charley Scobie within the hour."

"Sixty," Benton said. He shut his eyes, and they all knew he was contemplating a line of blue stretched painfully thin. But a moment later he said, "Do it."

Brautigan instructed his sergeants. Before releasing them, however, he turned again to Benton. "Marshal Scobie ought to delay the draft call," he said.

"What's the good of telling me a thing like that, John? You know Scobie as well as I do. By the book or nothing. Hell might freeze, but the draft will go on as scheduled."

116

"That bloody damn draft," Royce said. "Lincoln and his bloody draft are going to get us all killed before this is over."

"Jacob," Benton said, "is there a thing *you* might say to Scobie?"

Astor shook his head. "Not even if I held his mortgage. He's of that vanishing breed, an honest man." His voice went dry. "Like Royce here."

Royce kept silent.

"O'Neill," Benton said, "tell Captain Hilliard to do what he can to persuade Marshal Scobie. On your way, lads."

Brautigan crossed the room with Stephen. "Where to now?" he asked.

"My office. I have to report to Greeley. And then I suppose I will make my way to Marshal Scobie's where I suppose I will find you, won't I?"

"Yes."

But he seemed abstracted.

"It's going to be that bad, is it?" Stephen asked.

"About as bad as you can imagine. So bad we might want everyone we care about miles away from it if it can be arranged."

"Rosie and the boy are scheduled for the early ferry to Newark."

Brautigan tried to guard his expression, but relief wriggled past the outposts. An instant later he asked, "And Margaret?"

"There it seems the best I could do was send an urgent message to the orphanage."

In the tone and construction of this Brautigan sensed something worth pursuing, though obviously it could not be done just then. His hand, however, continued to bar Stephen's progress.

"Be careful."

Stephen smiled. "The pot calling the kettle black," he said.

117

3

Rosie, restless and with forty minutes to spare before the ferry was scheduled to leave, yielded to impulse. She left the sleeping Stephen Jr. in their cabin—Inga, the Jardines' housekeeper watching over him—and went back down the ramp to the wharf. She moved briskly, as if, unconsciously at least, the need was to outrace something. Which it most certainly was not, she told herself with some annoyance, checking her speed.

Corner of Rector and Washington streets. Well, there it was, looking smaller and dimmer than she remembered it. And yet, she decided a moment later, not changed all that much: Kerrigan's Grocery-Groggery. How her father had loved the place. And how she had loathed it; and loathed being made to wait there for him. ("Back in five minutes, Princess, and won't I be carryin' the gorgeous custard for my own heart's darlin'.") A mission seldom accomplishable in less than an hour.

She peered into the Rector Street window. It took a few seconds for her eyes to adjust to the gloom. Then she saw that the inside as well had fought off change. Two rooms: the nearer rectangle by far the smaller. On either side of this were hills of cabbages, potatoes, tomatoes, eggs, dried apples, chestnuts, and beans. In the valleys between were boxes of varying sizes and contents: nails, plug tobacco, candles, molasses, crackers, allspice, tea, ginger, and mustard in no particular order. And, interspersed—again in no particular order—bins of sugar and meal.

The crossbeams that supported the ceiling were centers of pungency, thickly hung with hams, tongues, sausages, and strings of onions. If you left Kerrigan's at noon, say, it would be half past one before you could safely swear you had not been there.

In the back, flanking the sides of a small green door, were ranged two long files of upright casks. Rosie recalled that the ones on the left were reserved for lamp oil and coal. But it was the ones on the right that got to the heart of the matter, the secret of her father's passion for the place. In these were brandy and whisky, most of which was manufactured by Kerrigan himself in that area behind the small green door where a huge kettle and a time-blackened furnace made the alchemy possible.

The larger rectangle, of course, was all saloon.

The grocery door fronted Rector Street; the saloon or groggery door Washington Street. Glancing up, Rosie wondered if the Kerrigans had ever repainted to restore the missing g in Groggery (lost—though they never knew it—through a piece of Michael Brautigan's pranksterism). She thought she might investigate and had just got underway when the door in question burst open. Three male figures flung themselves out onto the street: two boys of thirteen or fourteen followed by a third, somewhat older. In the next instant she experienced a click of recognition. No mere "third somewhat older." It was Michael himself.

Forebodingly she entered where the three had exited. Kerrigan, a small, frail man in his fifties, was alone in the room. He had been knocked down and was climbing shakily to his feet as Rosie came in. He looked at her, eyes distended in fright and then experienced his own click of recognition.

"Rosie Shannon?"

"Yes, Mr. Kerrigan. Your poor face. What's been done to you?" His fingers crept to the gash on his cheek and sprang back at

119

once as if the blood they touched was hot. "Moira! Moira! For God's sake, woman, come out here and see what's been done to me."

Rosie started to say something reassuring, but before she could get very far with it a back door opened, and a woman no taller than Kerrigan but considerably more robust appeared.

"What's all the clatter?" demanded Mrs. Kerrigan.

Kerrigan ran to her, losing himself in her commodious bosom. "They've killed me, Moira darling. The little bastards have gone and given me my death wound. See how the lifeblood's draining from me." Slumping against her, he finished softly, "Best get me to the hospital."

She held him from her the better to examine him. "Killed indeed," she said, letting her breath out in gusty relief. "A dozen like it and still no danger. All it needs is a wash. You're such an awful coward, Kerrigan. You grow worse as you grow older."

"It's true, it's true," he said meekly and allowed himself to be hurried toward the back room. But after three or four steps Mrs. Kerrigan suddenly stopped and whirled. "Saints alive, that's Rosie Shannon," she said.

"Yes, Mrs. Kerrigan. How are you?"

"How pretty you've got. Ain't she, Kerrigan?"

But having just seen on a pinky tip another specimen of his blood, he could only groan.

Mrs. Kerrigan's eyebrows shot heavenward. "A minute, Rosie, and we'll have ourselves a fine cup of tea. And a fine talk."

"I can't ma'am. I have the ferry to catch."

"Sure, and the next one would do as well, wouldn't it?"

"No, ma'am. I'm sorry."

"It hurts, Moira," Kerrigan whispered. "Saints, how it hurts.

"Well, then come along, little one, and I'll tend to you." She yanked him forward.

"Mr. Kerrigan," Rosie called after them, "was that Michael Brautigan I saw running out of the store?"

"Michael? Yes, yes, Michael Brautigan. Oh my God, how it hurts."

120

"Did he . . . ?"

"Yes, he did, by God!"

Rosie appropriated Margaret's "damn and blast" and muttered them under her breath. But a moment later there was Kerrigan shaking his head and saying, "Chased those little bastards away he did. Don't know what mischief they'd have made if it hadn't been for Michael. Would've done the chief inspector proud to see it."

The door shut behind them.

Grinning, Rosie retraced her steps to the wharf. Brautigan was there waiting for her. She started to run, eager to give him the gift of what Michael had done. When she got closer, however, she saw in him not the mirror of her own gladness, but the leftover of yesterday's *selflessness*. And this so irritated her it clean drove Michael away.

He glanced at her, did his own tallying up, and then, almost defensively, said, "The streets . . . I had to come down to see you off safely."

"Did you?"

"Ah, Rosie."

She attempted to brush by him, but he took her hand, halting her.

"Are you saying we can't be friends?" he asked.

"Are you saying we can be?"

"Why not?"

"Well, I will just write you a book about that. In the meantime I would be much obliged if you stood out of my way so I can go on about my business."

He moved aside.

"Thank you kindly."

After three or four steps, however, she stopped and came back. There was some blistering, absolutely excoriating thing to say, but she realized suddenly she did not know what it was. It was as if the ice floe around her heart had spread, managed so swiftly to work its way upward that both her brain and tongue were frozen.

In *his* face, too, she could read December.

121

But the chemistry of this was mysterious. It triggered a spurt of melting rage. How *dare* he be distant, as if the trap that was closing itself around them were anything but his fault.

"Fool," she said scathingly. "The bull in the china shop, that's what you are. You don't even know what you damage." And ran from him.

Anger freed him, too. Hot and flushed as she, he yelled after her, "Better sorry now, by God. Better now than later." And stormed away in his own right.

4

The air was lifeless. Swaying to the mesmerizing motion of a Third Avenue omnibus, Stephen felt all but lifeless, too. His eyes were heavy. In less than fifteen minutes his collar had thoroughly wilted, and sweat was a constant trickle down his back. At Thirteenth Street the track was blocked by an endless line of abandoned vehicles. Stephen shook himself awake, rose, paid his fare, and became a pedestrian. That was better.

And yet it was as if his short trip on the omnibus had transported him to a foreign city. From Twentieth on, for instance, every shop he saw was boarded shut. All the people he saw looked shut, too—small clusters standing, staring, waiting. (But for what?) Occasionally he heard a brogue (here a male, there a female) raised to condemn the bloody draft. But really nothing more riotous than that. No tangible signs of the ragtail army he had been warned about. No dramatic signs of the war it was reputed to be fostering. And for that matter, no evidence at all of police or soldiers.

At Forty-sixth Street, however, everything changed again. As he turned into it he saw the charred remains of three buildings. He recognized the vestiges of Brady's Saloon. A fire engine was stationed in front of it, energetically spraying water to no purpose, while a small crowd looked on, and, for some reason, applauded.

A few yards further up the street, he came on another small crowd in front of a three-story brick house that had once been gracious. It was so no longer. All its windows were broken, and still a squadron of small boys were heaving paving stones as if once patterned they could no longer stop.

The truly large crowd—about a thousand, Stephen estimated uneasily—was in front of the provost marshal's. He saw an occasional rifle, but many more axes, shovels, and makeshift clubs. To his surprise he had no trouble getting through. This was a settled rather than a milling crowd, he decided. An anticipatory crowd. It knew itself. It was a crowd infused with a sense of mission. Over and over again, almost like an incantation, he heard that by now familiar coupling: "Bloody draft. Bloody draft."

And everyone seemed to have a bottle. Here and there he saw men and women sitting on empty beer kegs. He saw one little boy giggling and washing his face in the soapy suds. Waiting, they were. All of them waiting. For what, he asked a big, somber-looking man who stood impassively with his arms folded across his chest and a thick, leather fireman's belt—buckle outward—wrapped around his enormous right fist.

"They say now they ain't going to be no draft," the man answered.

"Who is they?"

His glance remained fixed on the drawn blinds of Marshal Scobie's office. Then: "Doors still closed, ain't they? Supposed to begin at eleven. Half past that now, ain't it? Maybe there ain't going to be no bloody draft."

Brautigan let him in in time to witness Marshal Scobie's fury.

"Nobody . . . you hear me . . . I mean nobody . . . not the mayor, not the governor tells Charley Scobie how to do his duty."

From where Stephen stood he had an unimpeded view of the back of the provost marshal's neck. It could hardly have been

124

redder. Facing Scobie, towering over him, was a police officer Stephen thought he recognized.

"Is that Hilliard?"

"The very one," Brautigan said.

"Something of a martinet?"

Brautigan kept silent.

"Off the record," Stephen said.

"In that case you're looking at a matched pair."

"I'm not telling you how to do your duty," Captain Hilliard roared. "What I'm doing, Charley, is asking you to get over to that window and take a look at what's going on outside."

"I know what's going on outside."

"No, goddammit, you don't. I've been here half an hour, and you haven't looked out once. And I'm telling you it's worth a look."

Scobie, muttering something heated but unintelligible, moved to the window. In the meantime Stephen surveyed the interior. It was jammed with police.

"Exactly sixty-four of us," Brautigan said. "That ancient fire-plug of a man next to Captain Hilliard is Captain Moriarity of the Sixth."

"I know Captain Moriarity. He was your dad's good friend, was he not?"

"My godfather," Brautigan said.

"A mob," Scobie said. "That's all it is. A mob of cowards too chicken-livered to fight for their country. One touch of steel, and they'll run screaming. And so the question is . . ."

Hilliard drew himself up to become Goliath. He stared down at his David. But as to skin color, both faces were identically scarlet. "The question is . . . what?"

"The question is, is Barney Hilliard stout enough to give it to them?"

Moriarity got between them. An arm around each man's shoulder, he somehow contrived to move them apart and at the same time herd them toward the rear of the office, away from their audience. Out of earshot he carried on with what was obviously an attempt to defuse.

125

"Scobie says he'll wait until noon, no longer," Brautigan said. "Don't ask me what he expects to happen at noon because I don't know. Maybe he expects God to make a miracle by then, to reach down and show He's on the side of the righteous by dispersing the crowd."

"Will God be cooperative?"

Brautigan did not answer. But after a moment he said, "I take it as given that you absolutely have to be here, but this is no Hamilton School rugger game, do you understand? There isn't a single thing about that crowd out there I like."

"Yet it's such a quiet crowd," Stephen said. "Look at them. They're just standing around."

"When Charley Scobie announces what his duty compels him to do, I expect we'll see an end to standing around." He looked at Stephen hard. "I want you to believe me . . . it's important, Stephen . . . that's a mean quiet out there."

"I believe you."

"Good. Then I'm asking you to pay close attention to me now. At the far corner of the back room I've discovered a small door. One man only gets through it at a time, and that man crouching. It opens on an alley which in turn leads to mid-Forty-fifth Street. And the last time I looked, there was no welcoming party at the end of it. When it seems the sensible thing to do, will you remember that?"

"I'll remember it."

"Do I have your promise?"

"Come on now, John, don't bully."

A sudden roar from the crowd. About fifty yards away a man in a gorgeous white suit was being hoisted to a makeshift podium. It was formed from beer kegs and some wooden staves laid across for a floor.

"Who is he, do you know?" Stephen asked.

"I can make a pretty good guess."

And then Stephen realized he could, too. "The notorious Mr. Campfield," he said and was immediately borne out.

Beneficent smile. "My name is Campfield," the speaker said

126

and stopped when full throats acclaimed the announcement. He held up his hand and earned quiet. "Now some of you know me, and some of you do not, but that doesn't signify. What signifies is I speak for us all. I speak for my brothers. I speak for justice."

His voice was a marvel, Stephen thought. Rich, deep, and effortless. Touched with the lyrical. Touched with the South. But no one in his audience seemed to take that amiss. In fact they seemed to wallow in it, responding to it as if it were merely a more pertinent kind of brogue.

"What signifies is that in me you see no nigger-lover."

A roar.

"No abolitionist preacher come to tell you lies about what is right and what is wrong. What is sinful and what is virtue. What is brotherhood and what it never on God's earth was meant to be. Lies about what niggers want and what they don't. You know what niggers want?"

"Our jobs."

Campfield: "Wrong."

"They wants white women."

Campfield: "Wrong. And wrong. You think that's what niggers want? You are wrong, my brothers. And I am here to tell you how wrong you are."

"No, no, we ain't. We ain't wrong."

Soaring over them. "You could not be more wrong if you were to stay here all night. You know what niggers want? Shall I tell you?" His voice now dropped to a point where the words could not be heard without strain, but Stephen would have bet few in his audience missed them.

"Everything you've got," he whispered.

Stunned silence.

"They're going to come through here like the Baltimore and Ohio," Brautigan said. "Stephen, keep your mind on that door."

Extending his arm toward the provost marshal's office—as if to guide a lightning bolt—Campfield said, "There's the nest of nigger-lovers, the roost of vipers who want to tear good men from their families and send them out to die in an unholy war. Are you

127

going to stand for that? Are you going to let them have their way with you?"

"No, no. End the bloody draft."

"Marshal Scobie, do you hear that? Where are you, Scobie? We want you out here."

Hilliard and Moriarity had hold of him. Nevertheless Scobie, face flaming, had crossed the threshold of the front door, the two brawny bluecoats holding on for dear life.

"Charley, they'll crucify you," Moriarity said, teeth gritted.

"The hell they will. Nothing but a pack of cowards. And so are you, Tim Moriarity, by God, you are. Or you'd be out there breaking the head of that rebel son of a bitch. Listen at him, shooting his mouth off just like this was Richmond, Virginia. Turn me loose, dammit."

By this time the captains had help. Four bluecoats wrestled Scobie to the ground, and two of them sat on him to keep him there. But they could not keep him speechless.

"Cowards! Yellow-bellies!"

Moriarity came over to join Brautigan and Stephen. "The telegraph wires are down, you know," he said morosely to Brautigan. "All of them."

"I know."

Then they were both silent. Suddenly Stephen realized he was being given a cue. "Is there something I can do to help?"

Moriarity looked at Brautigan, who hesitated briefly but then nodded.

"Someone has to get a message to Two hundred Mulberry Street," Moriarity said. "It will have to be someone in civvies. Bluecoats ain't going to be able to get through that mob." He paused. "May not be easy for a civilian either."

"What message?"

"Just find the supervisor and tell him what's happening here. Not that it's a question of reinforcements, you understand. They would come too late. But from a reliable source headquarters has to know what's taking place." He cleared his throat. "But only the supervisor, Mr. Jardine."

128

"Not Royce is what the captain means," Brautigan said.

"The chief inspector ain't as discreet as his pa always told him he ought to be. On the other hand we wouldn't want you to be going to all the troubling for nothing."

"You've made yourself quite clear," Stephen said. "Shall I leave now?"

"No. In another minute or so we're going to have to turn that banty rooster over there loose. When the crowd reacts to that it figures to provide a useful distraction. Leave then. And good luck to you, sir."

Moriarity shook hands and returned to Scobie and his captors. Though his belly was still jammed to the floor—Captain Hilliard in the saddle—the provost marshal was engaged in an earsplitting exchange of taunts and insults with the rival champion.

Campfield: "You'll send men to die, but you won't come out and face them."

Scobie: "Liar! Scalawag! Oh God, strike him dead. Strike them all dead who stand between me and my duty."

And then suddenly Provost Marshal Scobie was on his feet and striding—short, quick steps through the crowd, to the podium itself. Shoulders squared, back stiff. With freedom he had recovered dignity. The crowd grew silent, let him through. Five yards from Campfield he stopped. They stared at one another, and just for the moment, the smaller man seemed to have become hunter when by all odds he should have been prey.

Booming. "In accordance with the National Conscription Law enacted March 3, 1863, I hearby state that the draft for the Ninth Enrollment District, sixth and seventh wards, New York City, shall commence as prescribed by regulation."

The last three words were drowned out. Stephen learned of them only later at the *Tribune* office—from Morrison, who had been one of a modest band of reporters tucked away on the west side of the podium. Drowned out by the anguished roar of the crowd. And yet, like something cemented, Scobie stood there, arms akimbo, mouth moving in silent shouts as hands reached toward him. A squad of bluecoats beat the mob by inches.

129

"Move," Brautigan said.

Stephen was reluctant.

Brautigan shoved him hard.

Stephen made for the rear door. Crouching to go through, he stopped for a moment to look back. The police were retreating to the inner office. Four lines deep, locust sticks at ready, they were preparing to repel attack. Stephen wondered if any had pistols. Then he saw that those in the front line did. Brautigan was one of them.

"Good luck," he shouted to him, though he knew he could not be heard.

The alley curved, then curved again, though less sharply. The effect of this was an acoustical cul-de-sac, so that Stephen exited into sudden quiet. Forty-fifth Street was like an oasis. But it was more than just the sound cut off that created the illusion. Forty-fifth Street was simply not at war. It was normal, orderly. It was New York on a typically hot July day, as if the madness one block south were chimerical. The contrast was stunning. As half running, half walking he made his way, people tried to stop him—but only for news. At Forty-first Street a huge old man in shirtsleeves and suspenders sat on his front steps crooning to a screaming baby.

"What's happening up there, lad?" he called to Stephen as he went by.

"Riot," Stephen called back.

The man nodded and went on with his song.

At the corner of Thirty-fifth, Stephen slowed to a brisk walk, maintaining that pace until he reached Second Street. There he picked up tempo again as he approached the Bowery. Right onto Walker; cross Elizabeth; then Mott, the street in back of the armory. He remembered the sequence for a long time. In fact he remembered it all his life, because it was just as he turned into Mulberry—within sight of his destination—that the thing came into view, though at first he could not identify what he was seeing. Or perhaps, he thought later, it was a case of his mind protecting

130

him, blurring the image to soften shock. Except that nothing could have really protected him.

A black man hung from the lamp post. He had been whipped, and his shirt was shredded, blood-stained. His trousers were gone. So were his genitals. And as Stephen fought back vomit, he realized that he knew him. Despite the swollen bruises on the face, the glassless spectacles hooked on one ear, the snowman's cigar jammed into the mouth, Stephen recognized Mary Haines's whorehouse piano player. As if to make some cosmic joke, he shared a currently famous name—Willie Jones, the name of the first man drafted.

By now the plate glass had gone, all of it, smashed by bricks and paving stones. Figures broke from the mob, dashed up to the front door, screamed obscenities, flaunted rear ends, then ran back, giggling. Some of these were men; some were women and children.

Hurrying along the front line, Moriarity tried to make himself heard. "When I fire, you fire," he roared into each man's ear.

Brautigan wondered where Hilliard was and then a moment later saw him on the floor in the back of the room. Unconscious. Blood streaming from a brutal gash over his left temple. A rock or a stone. His head was nestled in the lap of a man who dabbed at the wound with a handkerchief. Lap and handkerchief belonged to Provost Marshal Scobie.

Everything that happened next happened almost simultaneously. The door burst open. As much of the mob as could fit through the aperture came hurtling in, climbing on and falling over each other. Moriarity fired. Brautigan and the rest of the front line followed suit. Six bodies went down. Two were left there when the mob retreated.

After a moment Moriarity said, "They ain't panicking. I hoped they might, but it's not going to be. All right, there ain't going to be no mass suicide here. Everybody out the rear door. Easy now, single file. Some of you help Marshal Scobie with Captain Hilliard."

131

"Leave him be," Scobie said, voice flat. "He just died."

Moriarity hesitated, then nodded. "Chief Inspector, will you lead them out please?"

Brautigan got them started. When he had done that, when he saw them exiting as briskly as possible, he returned to Moriarity and squatted at his side.

"John, go with them," Moriarity said. "I'll be rear guard."

"We'll be rear guard."

Moriarity looked at him. "Big talker that you are. 'This is your show, Tim Moriarity.' Ain't that what you said? 'You give the orders, Tim, I'll obey them.'"

"Most of them," Brautigan said.

"Get us more pistols," Moriarity said.

Brautigan did, commandeering a half dozen from the metropolitans waiting their turn to exit. When he returned from the back room he found Moriarity carefully dividing his ammunition in two piles. Brautigan added to both, then filled his pocket with thirty or so rounds.

Moriarity said, "They making progress?"

"Halfway there. Maybe a little better than that."

"If we can hold those savages for five minutes after the last man's through, it ought to be enough."

Brautigan nodded.

"I thought they'd break and run, John. I mean in my gut I thought Scobie was right. Shoot the odd one down, I thought, and the rest would scatter like rabbits."

"Booze. Else they would've."

"No, not just booze. There's the anger, too. Righteous anger. Heady stuff. Beats the bejesus out of booze for making Brian Borus out of your ordinary bog-trotting, wife-beating Irish mick."

"Brace yourself," Brautigan said. "Here come the heroes."

Point blank range and hard to miss. Four went down at once, but it was a tidal wave. Retreating from it, they fired as they worked their way toward the back room, then to the tiny door. They found three men still waiting. Now all three tried to squeeze through at once, causing a jam-up. And fear froze them that way.

132

One was a boy under twenty, a recruit from the Eighteenth precinct. Brautigan recognized him but could not recall his name. His face was white.

"Shut the door," Moriarity shouted. "The rest of us stand and fight."

The recruit hesitated. Brautigan placed his foot against the youngster's backside and shoved him through. Then he shut the door behind him.

Moriarity said something to him that he could not hear. By now the noise was deafening. The mob was all over the place. The draft wheel had been smashed. As was every window. As was most of the furniture, smashed and indiscriminately thrown out into the street. He saw someone split Moriarity's head with an ax. He saw someone else pull a jar of cloudy white liquid from his pocket. Tom Green, the sixth precincter next to him, pointed and mouthed the words, "Greek fire."

Brautigan could not hear him either, but he did not have to. He smelled the sulphur even before the bottle hit the wall, exploding. Puddles formed. An instant later they became puddles of fire. An instant after that each connected and became a river.

Only Brautigan and Green were on their feet now. Engulfed. Cut off from retreat. Back-to-back and swinging their locust sticks in short, vicious arcs. Brautigan avenged Moriarity several times over. But he was arm-weary. He knew it was almost over. The flames crept closer. He saw the blow coming, coming so slowly he could admire the glow of firelight reflected in brass knuckles. Aimed at his temple. He had a whole year to avoid it. He moved, not quite in time.

133

5

The Reardon Paper Company stood four stories high on the west side of Forty-sixth Street. And it stood unmolested. Not so much as a scratch in any of its handome yellow bricks. Not so much as a crack in any of its one hundred twenty-four windows.

The reason for this was not complicated. Tyrell's mantle lay over it. Nor was the reason for *that* complicated, Stephen had more than once told Brautigan. Tyrell was Reardon's silent partner. He was also—in his capacity as president of the city's aldermanic council—Reardon's largest customer. Some sixty percent of the city's need for paper was satisfied by this Reardon product or that. In an editorial recently, Stephen had labeled the prices paid exorbitant. Privately to Brautigan, he insisted on the word fraudulent. As he invariably did, Brautigan had nodded and said, "Let me know when you can prove it."

Like Robbo Royce, Dennis ("Beau") Reardon could trace his origins to Chrystie Street. There the resemblance ended. He was tall, thin, impeccable to the point of dandyism. His collar was always stark white and brutally stiff. Boutonnierre always correctly displayed, mustache elegantly waxed. They made illassorted bookends, Reardon and Royce, positioned on either side of Tyrell. It was just the three of them on the roof. Down below and across the street, flames were enveloping the provost marshal's office.

"Never did care much for Charley Scobie," Reardon said, around a semistifled yawn.

"Dull fellow," Royce said.

"All that talk about duty. Lowered the tone of the neighborhood." Giggling.

And then both heads swiveled toward Tyrell to see if he was enjoying their performance. It was, after all, in his honor. Tyrell gave no sign. His gaze remained fixed on the burning building.

Reardon said, "What do you think, Robbo? Any of your fellow metropolitans still in there?"

"Dead ones."

"Dead and deserving of it," Reardon said. "Shooting down their own kind that way. An eye for an eye I always say. Don't you, Terence?"

Tyrell kept silent.

Royce, nervous, said, "Terence, Brautigan's not in there, I tell you. I would have seen him."

Tyrell kept silent.

"I'm getting down off here," Royce said. "It's hot as hell."

Tyrell made an impatient motion, dismissing him.

Royce mopped his brow and stayed put.

Reardon said, "Terence, I been meaning to talk to you about my sister's boy, Jamie. You remember Jamie. Likely youngster. He's—"

Tyrell went rigid, and Reardon cut off at once. All three leaned forward to watch two men come out of the building, coughing and sputtering. One was half carrying, half dragging the other.

"Holy mother," Reardon said.

A police van drew up to the pair below. Two sergeants—one huge, the other undersized—leaped off. Gently, carefully, they put the wounded man into the van. The other, the one who had helped him out of the building, climbed in after. The van moved off.

Tyrell watched it draw away. After a moment, without a glance at his colleagues, he left his vantage point and started back downstairs.

Royce and Reardon hurried after him. Reardon, barely moving his lips, said, "Want a piece of advice, Robbo?"

Royce didn't answer.

"Find out who the hell it was who couldn't leave Brautigan to feed the fire."

"I know who it was."

"Who?"

"Brautigan's brat."

6

Margaret awoke abruptly, disoriented. But that was less important than how awful she felt. Thick-tongued, gritty-eyed. Add to this a headache of an exquisitely punishing nature. When she could focus on the mantelpiece clock, it told her the time was just short of noon. Then the sight of Jemima Wilson's unconscious body on the bed next to hers, limbs flung in every direction, filled in the rest of the story.

God in heaven, what a night it had been. The children so sick; uniformly high fevers, vomiting, one of them screaming in pain. But not cholera, Peter had said finally, at about three this morning, and it had been like the commutation of a sentence.

She sat up. The savage inside her head objected, and, instantly, she fell back again, groaning. Once more she glanced over at Jemima. Jemima was naked. That was sensible. The room was a jungle. Through its one window, arrows of sunlight sliced into both their bodies. A moment later she realized she was no less sensible than Jemima. Her clothes were in a pile on a chair. With painstaking care Margaret forced herself to sit up again. This time the pounding was less severe. And then in easy stages she managed to get herself dressed.

"Margaret?" Peter's voice. "Effie has breakfast for you."

News of interest. Now that the headache had subsided a bit, she could consider other anatomical messages. Her last meal had been breakfast the previous morning, and she was ravenous. She glanced over at Jemima. Inert. Margaret decided to let her sleep.

Eggs and fried bread and lots of hot, strong coffee. Margaret pitched in ferociously. The other two did not much more than observe—Effie with approval, Peter somberly.

"The children?" she asked him.

Effie answered. "Birdie, she still a hot little baby, but the others done cooled off considerable. Dr. Mackenzie, he still worried about Birdie though."

"Birdie's going to die," Peter said tonelessly and left them.

Margaret found him in her office, at the window, in his customary staring-at-nothing position. "Damn and blast, but you're a boor," she said.

He shrugged and said nothing.

"How can you be like this? You were splendid last night? Are you ashamed of having been splendid?"

As if from a camera, he squinted at her, framing her face in the air. "Margaret Blanchard Jardine," he said. "Sit down all three of you and have a drink."

"I don't want a drink."

"The more for me then, but for God's sake, sit. You look like an indignant mother hen. You look like you're about to beat me to death with your outraged wings."

She sat. Neither spoke for a while. He was so difficult, she thought, so trying; so full of sharp edges and problematical areas. One always had the sense of being tested, and, often as not, being found wanting though the standard itself remained obscure. As the silence grew, she found herself studying him. He had one of those remarkable faces, she acknowledged. Nothing could make it commonplace. Get it tired, get it dirty, it remained compelling. Light blue eyes, high cheekbones, strong nose and chin. A face one might find in Scotland's highlands. Or, she supposed, on its highways, masked. At any rate there was a glamour to it that, while in Paris, she had tried periodically to capture on canvas, never succeeding. In fact it was when she finally recognized this as beyond her skill that she accepted the limitations of her talent—and came home.

He was conscious of her study. Usually it made him restless to be looked at that hard. Today he allowed it. She understood why. The kiss. In ways neither of them had yet sorted out, it had changed their rules. Knowing her well enough to have a sense of her thought processes, he offered the flask again.

"It blurs the edges," he said sardonically.

"I think you drink so much around me precisely because you know I hate to see you do it."

"I wonder if that's true."

"Why did you tell Effie Birdie's going to die? Why was it necessary to be so . . ."

"Truthful?"

"Brutal is the word I was searching for."

"Your definition. Brutality is the truth that does not happen to suit you."

"Brutality is the weapon you seem fond of using against your friends these days. Be careful, Peter. You are in danger of becoming a bully."

He did not get a chance to counter. The rock that came through the window ricocheted off the wall and struck her ankle. She cried out. At once he was at her side, pushing back her skirt.

"Are you all right?"

"Yes, yes, of course. What's happening?"

There was a tear in her stocking but just a small scratch above the ankle bone. He let his breath out in relief. Then he said, "Stay here while I go and see."

Another rock came flying through to skitter across the floor. At the same time, they heard the sounds of children crying out excitedly and the thud of footsteps in the corridor. Peter flattened

139

himself against the wall. He held the shade back an inch and peered through the broken window.

"What is it?" Margaret asked, feeling, for some reason, compelled to whisper.

The answer came raucously, from down below. "Black sons of bitches, come out of there before we burn you alive."

The door opened. Jemima. Her tongue kept flicking nervously at her lips, but her voice was steady. "What they want, Mrs. Jardine?"

"We don't know yet. Is Effie with the children?"

"She getting them all in central parlor. Nurses, too. She done sent me to you, to find out what they throwing rocks for?"

"Watch it!" Peter called out.

The rock this time hit the door only a foot or so above Jemima's head. She bent low and scurried over to Margaret, crouching next to her.

"I know one of them," Peter said, his tone flat. "We all do. He visited us yesterday."

Jemima clutched Margaret's wrist.

"I'm coming over there," Margaret said.

"All right, but stay low and be careful."

She crossed the room safely and was positioned next to him when the rocks came hurtling through again, a heavy volley accompanied by shouts and yells. The words were lost in the barrage, but all three knew what they were meant to convey.

Quiet once more.

Now Margaret could steal a look out the window, but nothing she saw was reassuring. There were at least a hundred people surrounding the orphanage. They were inside the picket fence, what was left of it. Men and women. Some children, too, running in and out of flower beds, destroying them. The vegetable gardens were already devastated. She could see faces quite plainly. All looked ugly, the female faces as menacing as the males.

She saw the bald-headed man, Evarts. He was dressed as he had been the day before. He saw her, too, grinned, made an obscene

140

gesture and danced from one foot to the other like some bizarre mechanical doll.

"I'm going to help Effie," Margaret said and signaled Jemima to join her.

Fifty frightened children were huddled together in the large recreation room they called central parlor. They were overseen by six nurses, all black, who must have been frightened, too, though few signs of this were evident. The children hugged teddy bears and a variety of dolls. Some carried blankets. A few had been napping and needed help getting dressed. The nurses moved in and out among them, soothing and caressing. Effie was posted in the center. In each of her arms there was a small black girl. A boy burrowed into her lap. When she saw Margaret she made a spitting gesture. "I done seen women out there," she said. "What they doing out there? Don't they have babies of their own?"

Margaret did not answer. She felt a twinge of shame that hers was the only white face in the room. In recompense she hugged the little boy in her own arms so hard she realized, belatedly, she must have hurt him. He did not cry out. He hugged back.

From outside she heard Peter's voice and hurried to the window.

"There's nothing for you here," he shouted. "Just children. Frightened children." And then, an unconscious echo of Effie, he added, "I see a lot of you who must be mothers. A lot of you who surely would not want to see children come to harm."

"Ain't never birthed no pickanin'," a woman's voice answered from the middle of the mob.

But he had struck the right note, Margaret thought. He had made them ill at ease. He had been standing at the top of the steps, and now he descended them, all five of them, unhesitatingly, barely a limp. He stopped just in front of Evarts, separated from him by a yard, no more.

"We've met before, correct?"

And the man half mesmerized by audacity—as they all were—acknowledged that this was so.

"Sergeant Evarts," Peter said, pointing to the sleeve that had

141

once borne stripes. "And a good one, too, I warrant, or I don't know leadership qualities when I see them."

Evarts nodded. He was beginning to belong to Peter. And if, from the back of the crowd, there had not come just then a loud female giggle, he might have continued so. But the first triggered a second. And a third. And then Evarts was his own again.

"Dog shit. You think I'm stupid, Major? I been humbugged by the best of them. I ain't one of your thick-skulled niggers. Out of my way, Major, unless you want my bullet. Told you yesterday. Never killed the major yet I didn't enjoy doing it."

Peter did back up a step, but only so that he could talk over Evarts' head. "What do you want in there? What can you hope to—"

"Goods," a woman called out. Margaret saw her at once, a big woman in a blue bandanna. Heavy-shouldered, red-faced. But sober. Peter spotted her, too, and, deserting Evarts, went toward her.

"What goods?"

"They got good stuff in there."

"Furniture?"

The woman turned so that she, too, could address the crowd. "Them little niggers are living better than we are. I say that ain't right."

Roars of approval.

Peter waited. Then, though he spoke loudly enough to be heard generally, he kept his eyes fixed on the big woman in the blue bandanna. "Take whatever you want," he said. "Give me ten minutes to get the children and their nurses out, and everything in the building is yours. What do you say to that?"

"Let the little niggers go," someone called out. "They ain't hurting nobody."

"Ten minutes," the big woman said to Peter.

Margaret turned from the window and hurried to direct the lineup of the children. She placed Effie and Jemima at the head, herself at the rear, and interspersed the other nurses strategically.

142

"Briskly now," she said as Peter joined them. "Effie, march them right out onto the Fifth Avenue. Don't stop for anything, understand?"

"Yes, ma'am," Effie said and instantly raised her voice in "Jeremiah's Boots"—which was their favorite recess marching song. Margaret and the nurses sang along, and then the children, raggedly at first, but very soon in full chorus. In a moment they were clear of central parlor and in the corridor heading for the exit.

"Eyes straight ahead," Margaret said. "Straight ahead now, my tiny babies. Keep a good line there, Emily. Joseph, I don't hear any singing from you."

The singing was what they needed. It was familiar and vigorous. It involved them and got them out of the building in good order. As the last child passed, Margaret reached for Peter's hand. "Thank you," she said.

He jerked his hand from her, hiding it behind his back before suddenly thrusting it at her again. "Look at the damned thing," he said. It was shaking. She held it against her cheek.

But as they emerged from the building, Margaret saw that Evarts and a dozen or so of his colleagues were in alignment on the bottom step, forming a barrier. It was clear Effie had tried to pierce it; she had been knocked sprawling. The children, big-eyed, were now motionless. They had stopped singing. Some of them began to whimper, the nurses doing their best to comfort. Margaret rushed to Effie to help her. Limping more pronouncedly now, as if the effort to camouflage had become more than he was capable of, Peter followed.

Evarts paid no attention to any of them. His eyes were on Jemima, had been from the moment she stepped clear of the building. He elbowed the man next to him. It was obvious Jemima had been a topic of general interest.

Like Evarts, all the cohort on the bottom step wore bits of cast-off army clothing. All were in some stage of drunkeness. All watched Jemima—hushed, fascinated.

Where was the woman in the blue bandanna? Margaret searched for her and found her pushed toward the back. Her

143

heavy shoulders were slumped. She had been superseded, defeated. She would be no help to them. Margaret screened the faces for some other source of aid. She saw nothing but savagery.

She heard Peter take a deep breath. "We had an arrangement," he said to Evarts.

"You can take the little niggers anywhere you want. Who's stopping you. She stays behind."

"She does not," Margaret said. "Never."

Evarts made a survey of her. Insultingly. Taking forever about it. "Careful. Might be we can use some white meat, too," he said.

Grins and elbow-nudgings. Partly, it was ludicrous, a burlesque. And that enabled her to keep her voice steady enough: "The man who touches me will pay heavily," she said. But even as she spoke a wave of nausea hit her and told her how frightened she was. She knew it was a group teetering on the thin edge of civilization.

"Effie," Peter said, "get the children moving. Margaret, go with them. Jemima, come to me."

Effie and Jemima moved to obey their respective commands, but Margaret, anger building, stayed put.

His voice was venomous. "Damn it, do as you're told."

Effie half dragged her along as she shepherded the children toward what had been the picket fence entrance until the marauders destroyed it.

"Stop," Margaret said. "I won't have it. Doesn't he see—"

"He sees," Effie said. "She sees, too. And there ain't nothing to be done about it. Except for staying by to help after they through with her. That and saving the children."

"And saving me," Margaret said, trying to free herself.

Effie nodded grimly. "You want us not to?"

"Jemima," Margaret said, calling back to her while struggling furiously to evade Effie's powerful grip. "Run, run!"

But there was no place for Jemima to go. They had hemmed her in. She made no response to Margaret's call. Nor did she look in her direction. She stood very straight in the protective circle of Peter's arm. Her glance, fixed on Evarts, excoriated him. But it did

144

not deter him. He started up the steps toward her, his intention to force her back inside. The crowd watched, rapt.

Colonel Bunce rode into the courtyard.

Margaret had never supposed she could actually faint, but now relief overwhelmed her. She was sick with it. Her knees buckled, and she slid to the ground. When she came to her head was in Jemima's lap. She heard her voice, crooning softly. She wanted to ask Jemima if she were really all right, only her vocal chords would not function.

But Jemima guessed. "I'm good, lady," she said.

Finally Margaret could talk. "How long . . . ?"

"Three, four minutes . . . that's all."

"Damn and blast," she said, fighting her way erect with Jemima's help. "Spectacle of myself."

"You was scared for me, lady."

"That is hardly an excuse." But then she squeezed Jemima's hand as hard as she could. She took a deep breath. "Did I really see . . . ?"

There was no need to finish because it was obvious she had indeed seen the roly-poly but, to her, majestic figure of Colonel Bunce on horseback, at the head of his squad of twenty or so blue-clad foot soldiers. They were still there. They formed a cordon around all of them—Margaret, Jemima, the children, the nurses, Effie, and Peter, too.

Not that much attention was being paid any of them now. It was odd, she thought. Everyone was faced away from her. It was as if, while unconscious, she had been whisked to a theatre and was now watching the play from backstage. Then her mind settled in. Over a trooper's shoulder, she watched what the rest watched, the orphanage being looted.

For the next ten minutes, in silence, they bore witness to a relentless pillaging. It was performed with gusto. And something like efficiency. No age bracket or sex went unrepresented as a steady stream of people denuded the building: parts of a piano, stair rods, books, chairs, teddy bears, pillow cases packed with silverware and crockery. Margaret saw a man wearing a hoop

145

skirt. (He lurched into a showy jig as he emerged from the doorway.) She saw a woman with a baby in her arms wearing Jemima's hat. She saw a drunken fight break out over a three-legged chair.

Colonel Bunce rode over to her and dismounted. "Animals," he said.

She found it difficult to tear her glance away.

"Dear lady," he said. "How splendid to see you on your feet again. And the roses back in your pretty cheeks. You are feeling better, I trust?"

She made herself give him the attention he deserved. "Yes, thank you, Colonel."

"Splendid, splendid. General Macklin will be so pleased when I tell him we were of service to the daughter of Henry Blanchard. He did so admire your late father. 'Never, Bunce,' he has said to me often, 'was our state better led than when Henry Case Blanchard governed.'"

Peter grinned derisively behind Bunce's back.

"We will be eternally grateful to you, sir," Margaret said, ignoring Peter. "I don't know what we would have done if you had not happened by just then."

"We did not just happen by, Mrs. Jardine. Oh, bless me, no. You have General Macklin's tactical genius to thank for our presence here. He has divided the Seventh into reconaissance commands, each leader with his designated sector of the city. Each charged by him to seek out insurrectionary behavior."

"Knight Errants all," Peter said. "General Macklin's Table Round."

Bunce was taken aback. He knew Peter well enough to distrust him intensely. Nevertheless, he could not help finding considerable charm in the figure. Knight Errants. General Macklin's Table Round. The general would be pleased, too, he knew, when he passed it on. He made a noncommittal throat-clearing noise as he restored his plump body to the saddle. He saluted Margaret with his riding crop and cantered off, bemused.

"Exit Sir Galahad jiggling," Peter said sourly.

146

She started to speak, but he cut her off. "Please no homilies. Let's agree that I'm beyond saving."

"Stuff and nonsense," she said. "Your behavior today—"

But again he prevented her from speaking. His face looked flushed, and perhaps because of that she thought his eyes looked dangerous. The drink, she decided. Or perhaps the aftermath of the melodrama they had just lived through. Or heat from both. At any rate, suddenly there was the sort of wildness about him that recalled milestones of her growing up. She saw them in flashes: the mad drive over the snow, outracing her fear of death; the absurd and yet equally terrifying night when—arrogance matched against innocence—he had tried to take her to bed. As a matter of principle, he had said. Without—or at least before—benefit of clergy, the approval of state, and the blessings of Blanchards.

Had he been serious? In retrospect, she thought not; not to start with. It had been, she thought, little more than a demonstration of what a cosmopolite Europe had made of him. Also, it was a way of teasing her. But the effect on her—unsophisticated as she was then—had been larger than he had anticipated. She had reacted as if he were a monster, and this had so taken him by surprise that he found himself with a situation he had no idea how to manage. That infuriated him, made it somehow necessary to press an attack. A child and frightened, she had run from him to the safety of a world in which Blanchards were, to a degree, sacrosanct.

"Come, Margaret," he said now, "we have unfinished business."

The words and tone were mocking, but the challenge— legitimatized by an unrepudiated kiss—was issued to a grown woman and in dead earnest.

147

7

From Stephen Jardine's diary. Monday, July 3:

. . . so much *casual* destruction. The same fire that took Charley Scobie's office, for instance, consumed these innocents as well: Quimby's (combs, brushes, etc.); Peel's (carriages); Newman, Onderdonk & Ciphron (hardware); Jewett's (jewelry); H. Brady (saloon): half a block of noncombatant tenements and other harmless dwelling places, new and old, large and small. Value: an astronomical $90,000.

The mayor has issued a proclamation: "The laws of the City of New York must be enforced, peace and order maintained, and the lives and property of all its citizens protected at any and every hazard. I therefore call upon all persons engaged in insurrectionary behavior to retire to their homes and employments, declaring that unless they do so at once, I shall use all the power necessary to restore the peace and order of the city."

We are at war. With our own people. A civil war within a civil war. Throughout this terrible day and night reports to that effect kept coming into the *Tribune*, brought by *Tribune* stringers and a variety of volunteer messengers as well. All on foot. (Not a telegraph wire remains uncut.) We learned that: on Eleventh Avenue the tracks of the Harlem Railroad have been obliterated, block after block. Between Twenty-eighth and Twenty-ninth on Broadway, there is no street left. To make missiles, the mob-army has torn up the sidewalks.

Looting is the great pastime, and every gun shop, every grog shop was emptied before midmorning. An hour before I left the office, old Seth Crampton came in to tell Greeley, tearfully, that his family manse had been ransacked, then burned. (All those big houses on Lexington Avenue have been under attack.)

The ferry flips are vacant. No boats in the harbors. On East Forty-fourth Street, the Bull's Head Hotel is gone, gutted. The cattle in the stockyards were deliberately stampeded, and on any given city street, you can find a cluster of half-mad steers running this way and that. Like their half-mad liberators.

Riot, rampage, slaughter. Fires unfought and out of control. It is now a little past midnight, and as I look out my bedroom window I see a sudden blaze of light here, another there. And I know something huge is burning to the north of me.

From Broadway south to Bond Street and north to Union Square, no shop is without its iron shutters grimly in place. That territory belongs to the mob-army. None but rioters walk those streets unafraid. Nevertheless, only a portion of the island, to now at least, has been a battleground. Lucky Gramercy Place still slumbers peacefully tonight.

And, for that matter, all in the city are lucky who were clever enough not to be born black. Blacks are the mob-army's special prey. Not that there are all that many left to prey on. The exodus is general. Of yesterday's ten thousand, hundreds have fled to Brooklyn. Many more to New Jersey to hide in the woods there. Still more have been seen on the Hudson River Railroad tracks, making their way north. To where? Albany is the consensus. On foot. They carry what belongings they can.

Oh God, poor Willie Jones. Still, he hangs. Mob-army contingents guard his body like a captured battle flag. Every now and

149

then, police squads venture out to try to cut him down, but they are driven back.

The brutality is unbelievable.

Robinson saw a black man beaten with iron pipes, then chased to the pier at the foot of Oliver Street, then forced to jump. He drowned in eight feet of water. Both his arms had been broken, and he could not swim. The mob crowded to the edge of the pier, cheering his efforts until these gave out.

Morrison witnessed the hanging of a seventy-year-old woman.

Busby saw a black baby tossed out of a third story window.

And it was women, John Brautigan says, who mutilated Willie.

Greeley, munching apples at a rate that threatens even his mighty supply, paces. Seethes. Rages. Disappears to write an editorial. Emerges to read it to us. Tears it up—not scathing enough—disappears to write another. More or less I do the same. As does Morrison. Busby does not. By 4:00 P.M. he had drunk himself into insensibility.

Eleven good men died at Charley Scobie's . . . or just outside it . . . including poor old Tim Moriarity, Barney Hilliard, and Charley himself.

John has naught but a headache. A lesser head would have split in two, I told him—when Doc Briscoe unwrapped strips of Michael's shirt from it, and we could see what there was to see. A bruise of the highest pitch. Colorful and generously proportioned.

Hammer an Irish noggin, Brautigan said, and 'tis the tool that suffers.

He could not stop grinning.

Observing this, Briscoe warned that John would have to be watched; head wounds can cause bizarre behavior, he said.

I had a better diagnosis and kept it for this journal. It is that John would take two such cracks . . . bigger cracks, uglier bruises . . . if he could be certain it would lead to rescue by Michael.

I am bone weary but cannot sleep. This pen keeps moving obsessively.

How many other insomniacs are in this city tonight? Thousands upon thousands, I warrant, wondering if the mayor's pleas for help have reached the governor. If so, wondering if the governor's pleas for help—assuming he sent any—have reached Washington. Wondering if Lincoln has any troops that are not chasing Lee. And if he does, can they possibly get here before the city is in cinders? And wondering what dreadful sights our red-rimmed eyes will look upon tomorrow.

Margaret. I have just come from fixing her coverlet. No insomniac, she. The sleep of the utterly exhausted. Even so, how beautiful she looked. And young. And supremely innocent, her hair haloing on the pillow.

A nightmare, that scene at the orphanage. Peter, she says, was heroic. Peter is always heroic. A fish swims. A bird flies. A lion is fierce. An owl hoots at night, and Peter Mackenzie is heroic. It is in the nature of things.

Tuesday
July
4,
1863

1

How dispiriting to think of the glories of Independence Day during these inglorious times—James Gordon Bennett notwithstanding. Stephen glanced down again at yesterday's *Herald*, which Greeley had left on his desk, the editorial heavily circled. In it Bennett had made a flattering comparison between the civilian populations of both eras—Colonial and contemporary— in terms of a willingness to sacrifice in behalf of the war effort.

"Liar," Greeley had scrawled in the margin. "Heroes on the one hand, scum on the other."

As usual, when the publishers of the *Tribune* and the *Herald* took positions, they were at opposite extremes, and Truth, having no choice, lay somewhere in between.

Stephen got up and went to the window. If it would only rain, he thought, staring out at the Independence Day dusk, it might reduce body temperatures to a degree commensurate with rationality. A thunderstorm might send the *Tribune's* besiegers skedaddling. Actually, he would settle for just one bolt of lightning in the hope it might be construed as an act of God.

But the furnacelike sky remained inactive. Red and orange streaks. If one touched that sky, it would scorch one's fingers. An angry, portentous sky. But which side was in disfavor?

As he moved away from the window, he crunched glass under his feet. There was glass everywhere. This was by now a recognized concomitant of a mobocracy attack. They loved breaking windows. The sight and sound of it appeased their hunger for beauty, he decided sourly. Ten large windows on this side of the *Tribune* building, nine panels each—every one of them broken during the first two onslaughts. Result: not two square feet of office space without its tinkly overlay.

He heard Greeley, irritatedly, calling his name.

"Just on my way, sir," he said.

He would have to be on guard to keep his own irritation from showing. Greeley's irritation was unfocused—the result of a long wearisome day. Stephen's was focused on Greeley.

He had not fully entered—one foot was still in the corridor— when the publisher, heaving his apple in the direction (only the direction) of the trash basket, began a reading. The editorial was, of course, vitriolic. Its four predecessors that day had been no less so. Full of terms like running amok, primordial behavior, atavistic barbarians. Never mind that the chances of publishing a paper grew less by the minute. Never mind that the atavistic barbarians had been screaming for his hide since midday, six hours now. Why didn't the stubborn old man go home? If he did, the atavistic barbarians might, too.

"No man," Greeley descanted, "whatever his calling, can afford to live in a city where the law is powerless. This mob must be crushed. Every day's, every hour's delay is big with evil. Today, twice, they attempted to overrun us, that rabble, but they found us ready for them—forty-seven reporters and sixteen printers armed with nothing but righteousness and courage. And we beat them back. They are bullies. They are to be confronted, defied, grappled with, prostrated and crushed. It is true that there are public journals who try to dignify this mob. The *Herald*, for instance, characterizes it as the *people*; refers to them as the *laboring men* of the city. These are libels that ought to paralyze the fingers that penned them. People? No. They are damned, demented dogs. Shoot them down, I say."

He looked at Stephen, waiting for comment.

"I like the alliteration," Stephen said.

Greeley howled. He slammed the paper on his desk. "I want to scorch them. I want them to read this and fear damnation. And you tell me it alliterates. What in thunderation is wrong with you, Jardine?"

"Perhaps I'm tired, sir."

"Tired? You dare not to be tired. Pray, sir, look at me. Am I tired?"

Stephen obeyed his instructions and then said, "Apparently not."

"Do you wish me to be tired?"

"Since you ask, yes, I do."

"Pray, sir, tell me why."

"Because if you were tired you might do the sensible thing and go home. Colonel Bunce agrees with me, sir. If you went home, our besiegers might go home."

"Don't quote Bunce at me. A tin soldier. And his master, General Macklin, another one. And besides, if you've been listening, it's 'Bloody Butcher Bunce' they've been screaming for more than 'Nigger-loving Greeley.'"

Stephen slumped down on a chair and kept silent.

"Isn't that so?" Greeley demanded.

"The fact is Bunce can give you an armed guard to safety."

"Oh come now, Jardine, you exaggerate the danger."

"I do not, sir."

"Then ask Bunce to give you an armed guard."

"It's not me they wish to hang to a sour apple tree. And the like."

Greeley milked his muttonchops while his fierce blue eyes took Stephen's measure. "Would you turn tail before them?"

Stephen wanted to say yes and couldn't. The lie stuck. He said nothing. Greeley beamed. "I know my man," he said.

157

Bunce came in. "They seem to be massing for action. One contingent on Nassau and Spruce streets, the other on Park Place. Rather formidable arrays."

"They've massed before," Greeley said, "and we've turned them back."

Bunce seemed a shade nervous, surprising Stephen. During the course of the day, Stephen had concluded that the colonel, whatever his faults, was simply impervious to physical fear. But this time, though he smiled appreciatively at Greeley's bomast, there remained between his eyebrows a small *v* of concern. It made him look almost human, Stephen thought.

"General Macklin has ordered me to be personally responsible for your safety, sir."

Well, that explained it, Stephen thought. To Bunce, Macklin's orders had a sacerdotal quality. "Is it still possible," Stephen asked, "to escort Mr. Greeley from the premises safely?"

Bunce looked thoughtful.

"I had in mind through the basement to Windust's restaurant and out the back, beyond the crowd, on Park Place," Stephen said.

Bunce lighted up. "Excellent, sir. Excellent."

But accompanying this, Greeley was shaking his head. "I will not go," he said. "Jardine, get it through your obstinate skull. I *cannot* go." And then, grandly: "Greeleys do not desert."

Bunce's eyes glistened with admiration. "Splendid, sir. If only the general could have heard those words, how they would have cheered him in his sickbed. How they would have restored his faith in New York City's leadership." He snapped to attention and saluted Greeley smartly. "I must see to my troops, sir. In the meantime, sir, permit me to assure you on behalf of Squadron C, Troop F, Seventh Regiment that we will defend you to the last man." Slamming the door with Prussian severity.

Rising wearily, Stephen made to follow Bunce.

"Where are you going?" Greeley demanded.

"To see to my troops."

"Stephen . . ."

Only once before could Stephen remember Greeley referring to

158

him by his first name. That had been the day of his son's birth. Then, as now, Stephen had been caught unprepared.

"There's no reason for both of us to remain," Greeley said and raised his hand when Stephen started to reply. "It's my newspaper, my building. In other words, my ship. That being the case, I am compelled to take the action I take. Nothing compels you."

"I can't go if you stay," Stephen said.

A hard yanking at the muttonchops. "There is Margaret and my godson."

Stephen kept silent.

"This is most foolish of you, sir. I invite you to reconsider."

"And I invite you, sir, to join me on a trip through Windust's."

They stared at each other, neither giving ground. But then finally, with some hauteur, Greeley said, "At least urge our people to safety."

"I was on my way to do that, sir."

Greeley nodded.

Stephen resumed his progress.

"Jardine . . ."

He halted again. Greeley was staring out the window. "Look at them," he said, "the mobocracy. Howling like mad dogs. Drunken, debauched. What do they want of me? What did I ever do to them but strive to make their conditions better? They love Tyrell, who steals from them. They love Bennett, who panders to the worst in them, patronizes them, secretly despises them. But Greeley, who has grown old and tired in their service, him they want to hang. Why is that, Jardine?"

"I don't know."

"Of course you don't." But then, still without turning, he said, "You're a hardhead, Jardine. And there are times when you irritate me beyond measure. You have that knack. But I stopped you because I wanted you to know . . ." He broke off, reached for and polished a fresh apple, and then resumed. "In the event something does happen of an untoward nature . . . against that possibility, sir, I wanted you to remember I never met a man I liked better."

159

"Thank you, sir," Stephen said, managing not to miss a beat and to keep his voice perfectly steady.

"Now get out, get out."

And Stephen left—thinking that until the day the old man released him he would remain under Greeley's spell.

On his way to the pressroom, he detoured to reconnoiter. Down below it was obvious something big was getting ready to happen. The noise level was an indicator. All day it had been such—waxing before an attack, waning immediately after. In addition the mob was alive with torches. That in itself was not new, since in both previous attacks they had tried to set fire to the building. Once, in fact, they had been partially successful, but a Bunce counterattack had driven them off before the fire could really catch hold.

Now, however, there were so many more out there. No more than fifty strong at noon, now the mob numbered at least three hundred. Stephen continued toward the pressroom on the run. He had gone no more than a dozen steps when a mighty shout drew him to a window again, and he saw that the mob was surging toward the building. And then, while he watched, as suddenly as the attack had begun, it aborted. Stephen was shocked. It was the front row cracking back on itself like the coiled tip of a whip, and Stephen from his second-story perspective could see the devastating effect this was having. Bodies falling, entangling, scrambling free, and then—to his astonishment—joining unanimously in panicky flight.

He couldn't see what was causing it. Whatever it was was just beyond the range of his vantage point, seemingly at the foot of Park Place, hidden from him by one of the *Tribune's* huge green awnings. Hurriedly, he moved three windows down, closer to the pressroom, and then he saw it—or them, rather: a pair of snub-nosed nine-pounders, each manned by a squad of four civilians. One shiny black cannon was pointed toward Park Place, the other menaced Nassau and Spruce. Apparently, they had just been wheeled into place. But from where on earth had they come?

160

At any rate they looked formidable, and the crowd was reacting accordingly.

Bunce was jubilant. "General Macklin to the rescue once more," he said. "From his very hospital bed, he has managed somehow to save us."

"I don't think so," Stephen said.

"Sir?"

"I don't think it's General Macklin we have to thank."

"Most assuredly it is, sir. Those are U.S. Army cannon, and so marked."

"U.S. Army they may have been, but they seem to have changed ownership."

Greeley, apple core clenched in his teeth, burst from his office. "What happened? They're skedaddling."

By this time the corridor was jammed with reporters and pressmen making the same observation.

"Who is our benefactor? Does anyone know?" Greeley demanded.

"Good day to you, Horace."

Peaked artilleryman's cap tilted over his good eye, the speaker lounged smilingly against the wall near the pressroom entrance, and not a soul there doubted for an instant that he embodied the answer to Greeley's question.

Greeley stared.

"Bennett," he said wanly, the kind of tone men have always reserved for their least rewarding moments.

"None other," Bennett said.

After an exquisitely drawn out interval, during which all there felt his pain, Greeley said, "I owe you a debt of gratitude. Quite possibly I owe you my life."

"Thank you, Horace. Gracefully done."

And then, surprising them all, Greeley's knees buckled, and he sagged to the floor.

161

2

Listening to Greeley's gentle snoring, Stephen recalled the last days of his father's illness, in this very hospital. For two weeks, day after day, that sound had been Robert Jardine's most obvious sign of life. Desperately, Stephen had wished for one waking moment, one instant's release from coma so that they could say good-bye, but it had not come. In its place, in the middle of an evening as hot as this, had come instead the sudden shock of silence. Death here and gone while Stephen drowsed in his chair.

"The muttonchops, I guess. That's what makes him look so much like old Robert."

Stephen had sensed Peter at his back even before he spoke. Nor was the allusion a surprise. "I've often thought that," Stephen said. "Seems as if he's going to be all right." Turning to Peter for confirmation.

"Exhaustion more than anything else," Peter said. "When you brought him in, I thought he might have had a stroke. But it wasn't that. He just took more of a hammering than he could readily cope with, and his body called a halt."

"It's a wonder mine doesn't, all things considered," Stephen said, hauling himself erect. "I'll let him sleep now and come back later."

Peter went to Greeley's bed and gently adjusted the sheet, which had become twisted between the old man's legs. He took a while with that. When it was smoothed to his satisfaction, he said, "I've been thinking about a certain day. I don't know why, but for some idiotic reason it's found a crevice in my brain, and I can't dislodge it." He glanced at Stephen as if to invite comment, received none, and continued. "We were going fishing. It was supposed to be just the three of us—you, me, and your father. But somehow Margaret queened her way in. And then absolutely refused to bait her own hooks. Which made you furious because, as you kept insisting, that wasn't what fishing was all about, and no one had asked her there in the first place. Do you remember any of that?"

His gaze had become intense, challenging.

"Not in just that way," Stephen said.

"In what way?"

"I remember baiting her hooks—and you being unbearable to her."

"And you comforting her?"

"Yes."

He smiled. "I yield the point at once. It certainly does sound truer to type, doesn't it? But I swear to you it was in my mind as I told it. I wonder why."

He lifted Greeley's wrist, took his pulse, and then fixed the sheet again. He remained at bedside, motionless. Stephen realized there was no flask bulge in his pocket. That meant he was out of it, over it, in the dry segment of his cycle where he would stay until some blow to his equilibrium—or to his self-esteem— required brandy to restore the balance. It could be a month, it could be six. Peter turned. "A part of me has always wanted to be good," he said. "Like you."

"Like me?"

"Don't deny it. Stephen Jardine's goodness is a matter of universal agreement, an article of faith."

163

"All right, but then a part of me has always wanted to be like you."

"That's because evil fascinates good people."

Stephen took careful aim. "In your case, naughtiness, I would have said."

Peter cringed. "Oh God," he said. "Give me back evil."

They smiled at each other—old friends. A relationship in some ways deeper than any. Even when bitterness has begun a corrosion. Then Peter said, "I wonder if you ever understood how much I loved your father."

"I think I did."

"Did you? And how hard I tried to appropriate him?"

"Even a little of that. Given the circumstances I never thought of it as unnatural."

Peter kept silent, studying him. "It occurs to me that I may not deserve a friend like you. Has that occurred to you?"

"Often," Stephen said.

"And so it should have," Peter said. But when he raised his glance to Stephen's, it was direct and unequivocal. "And yet the plain fact is I'd never willingly do anything to hurt you."

Willingly. When he left the room the word still hung in the air.

3

" . . . Savages. With whom the gallant though overwhelmed forces of law and order have so bravely tried to cope. Savages? No, not savages. Howling devils. They claim principle, but in truth are goaded by greed and envy. A mob of trashmen and draymen, lamplighters and chimney sweeps—seizing the opportunity for unrestricted plunder. And rape. And murder. And every kind of sadistic violence. And call it the will of the people, if you please. Will of the people indeed! Better say will of the hun!"

Brautigan let the *Tribune* (a four-page shadow of its eight-page self) drop to the floor. He shook his head. No matter what else you might conclude about old Greeley, you could not doubt his courage. It was a clenched fist of an editorial—in the face of a populace that already detested him, had always detested him. And yet Greeley never seemed to understand that. Bennett was the people's choice, but Greeley thought *he* was. He woos the public, Stephen had once said, as if it were a bluestocking. While everybody else knows it's a whore. Brautigan grinned. Stephen and Greeley. No one could irritate Stephen more intensely than

Greeley. And yet Stephen's loyalty to the old man was unswerving.

Which led him to recall what Stephen had once said to him about Rosie, that from childhood she had always been one for the stray cat, the crippled doll, and the like. Let the decision in its favor be made, and the bond was forged. Yes, true, and, in fact, the rub. What tortured him so, what he had tried in his hapless way to convey to her, was rooted right there. It was the fear of having to *watch* her be loyal, the fear of seeing her, some day, imprisoned by commitment itself with nothing but iron years of discipline and nobility to face. He thought of her—the tones of her in his ear, her motions in his nerves, and the colors of her filling his sight so that he printed her on the air whenever he turned, as one does with a vivid light after looking at it. He made himself stop. Enough. It was over. Life went on.

And along those lines there was a situation of some urgency to deal with. Question: How long could he keep his own collection of "howling devils" at bay?

Because it was a curious siege they were under. It consisted of several hundred of the devils parading up and down Mulberry Street and not a solitary devil on Mott Street. So that all night, police and civilians had entered and exited that way at will. While anyone trying to do the same via Mulberry Street met a vicious volley of paving stones.

At one point Brautigan had given thought to why this lopsided besiegement. He decided it had something to do with Willie Jones, whose corpse had, inexplicably, become a prize of war; something to do with the absence of a devil-in-command, and a good deal to do with drink. Then he stopped thinking about it, forced to concern himself with one or another of the logistical problems that accrue when events transform a police headquarters into a combination fortress, hospital, and general sanctuary.

Brautigan retrieved the *Tribune* in order to pass it on to Doc Briscoe. Then he stood up from the cane chair that had been his bed and stretched painfully, thinking that every one of his veteran bones had been belabored. Gingerly, he touched the bruise on his

166

head and whistled at its tenderness. It had been a long night. He had had very little sleep. His eyes were puffy, his beard scratchy, and his throat rough with the warning of a miserable summer cold. He felt as if he were drowning in coffee, and yet at the same time wanted another cup. He went to get it from the woman volunteer, whom he first had to awaken.

"Another beastly hot day," she said glumly as she ladled from the huge, sterling silver vat bearing on it the legend, "A gift from a grateful T. B. Tyrell." The police force, that year, had been one of several New York institutions to which the Boss had shown gratitude on a sliding scale.

Mrs. Nolan was in her late thirties. When she had entered headquarters fifteen hours earlier, she had been a sprightly, solidly built woman with an obvious zest for the task she had set herself. Now she looked like her own mother, Brautigan thought sympathetically.

"Yes," he said. "No rain in sight."

"Not at all," she said. "Not a drop. And that's what they need, the ruffians. A dousing. Cold water, Chief Inspector. Nothing like it to shrivel a man, I always say."

Perhaps she saw an image of thousands of once full-sized ruffians reduced to miniatures by therapeutic cascades. At any rate she smiled. "Look at this place," she said, new energy in her voice. "Chief Inspector, what would you say if I rounded up a squad and did a job of spit and polish on it?"

"That I'd be forever in your debt, ma'am."

Off she went in search of colleagues as interested in bringing order to chaos as she. He glanced about him. It was indisputable that 200 Mulberry Street looked vastly unlike the neat orderly police center in which he took so much pride. Nor was that surprising.

All night long metropolitans had straggled in as precincts closed down throughout the city. Soldiers, too. Many of them wounded, some gravely. Going from casualty to casualty, the doctors had stitched and bandaged—bandaged and stitched until the air hung heavy with the smell of liniment and carbolic acid.

167

Debris covered the floor. Bits of torn newspapers, magazines, bloodstained clothing. And covering the floor, too, were people—policemen, soldiers, the orphanage children and their nurses, women volunteers from the neighborhood—three hundred souls in every nook and cranny of the armory. They were taking their toll. Brautigan looked down at the once unmarred black walnut floor. Hobnail boots had lacerated it. Tobacco juice formed an unending chain of sticky little islands. He knew how unimportant that was yet, momentarily, it depressed him. His glance fastened on a tobacco juice archipelago and would not be pried away. As he sipped his coffee, he let his breath out heavily. Stretched out on the cot that had been set up for him in his office, Supervisor Benton was still asleep. Doc Briscoe was changing the dressing on his shoulder, and though Brautigan caught only a brief glimpse of the wound, it was enough to make him anxious.

"Am I wrong, or does it look worse now than it did last night?" he asked.

Briscoe was a short, stumpy man about Brautigan's age. He had been a police surgeon almost as long as Brautigan had worn the uniform, and the two men got on well despite the doctor's famous short fuse.

"You are wrong," he said. "And I'll thank you to stick to your last." Then he relented. "Probing around for the bullet irritated the wound some, but it's out now, and he'll be all right. Which is more than he deserves, the old fool."

This was a reference to the manner in which the supervisor had received his wound. During the first of the several fruitless skirmishes around Willie Jones's corpse, the supervisor had positioned himself in the vanguard of a ten-man charge. He had done this over Brautigan's vigorous protest. ("Anyone can see they're without firearms, John.") He had gone no further than a dozen feet before a bullet knocked him back half of that.

Briscoe straightened. "I gave him some morphine," he said, "and he'll rest comfortably for a while. What are the chances of me leaving here without being torn limb from limb? Could use some more supplies."

168

"Mott Street's still open. Ten minutes from now, who knows? There's brave talk out there of burning us out."

"Talk only?"

"That's my guess. They lack the weapons, thank God, because they sure don't lack for people. Must be five hundred of them. On the roofs and all over the place. But only a handful of firearms, near as I can reckon."

By this time, Briscoe, bag packed, had quick-marched to the Mott Street door, Brautigan in pursuit. And pursued in turn by the impromptu police guard of four he had marshaled along the way.

"What's this?" Briscoe demanded, becoming aware of the formation trailing him.

"Shut your mouth, Doc, and do as you're told. Keep in mind that around here I outrank you."

Briscoe grumped something but gave signs of preparing to be tractable. Pleased, Brautigan leaned forward to open the door and found himself confronted by a narrow-eyed stare that sent warning signals clanging brainward. The stare belonged to a young black man who had been about to open the door from the other side. As a result the two faces were separated by less than six inches. Brautigan drew back. The other, grinning, followed suit. Brautigan was not fooled by the grin. It was companion to the stare.

Brautigan could now see further into Mott Street. There were about twenty or so other blacks strung out in a ragged line, four men and the rest women and children. At the head of the column was a man he knew, Reverend Dawson. He guessed the girl flanking him was Dawson's sister. When Dawson saw him, he nodded and smiled warmly enough, but he did not come forward. Brautigan decided that was Dawson's way of underscoring who their spokesman was.

But the spokesman did not speak. In torn and dirty clothes clearly not his own, he waited. Brautigan, who would have welcomed Dawson instantly, found himself irritated. Was waiting the game? Two could play at it. It became a war of nerves. Finally,

169

Dawson had no choice but to come up the stairs to join them. The young woman followed.

"Good morning, Chief Inspector. Morning Dr. Briscoe."

So intent had he been that Brautigan had forgotten Doc was still there. Silence was not typical of Briscoe, but he, too, was reacting to the warrior black. Briscoe's intensity made Brautigan try to tone down his own.

"Morning Reverend Dawson," he said. "And Miss Dawson. It is Miss Dawson, isn't it?"

She nodded and smiled. Despite the fatigue that marked her face, she was extremely pretty. Having noted this, he next noted how the young man's eyes flickered. That rekindled Brautigan's annoyance. He felt the back of his neck grow warm. What did he think Brautigan had in mind, rape right here on the armory steps?

Reverend Dawson smiled patiently.

In response, Brautigan took another tuck in his temper.

"Chief Inspector, this is . . ." Dawson hesitated only briefly, but long enough to make Brautigan wonder. ". . . my friend Richard Frazier from Boston."

Neither offered a hand; both nodded. A process that was repeated when Dawson introduced Briscoe.

It was Dawson who put out his hands—palms up, as if subconsciously he were asking to have them filled. "We are hungry," he said. "And tired. We need a safe place. Can you offer us that, Chief Inspector?"

"Of course." He stepped back from the door.

Briscoe said, "Think I'll stay for a while, John. Some of those pickanins look like they could use help."

Frazier now spoke for the first time. A mock whisper. "Pickanin, Cora," he said. "Dat mean baby."

Reverend Dawson shook his head admonishingly, but Frazier looked unadmonished. Suddenly, Brautigan thought he understood what was happening. There was a feverishness to Frazier, a kind of overwrought excitement he thought he recognized. He guessed he was watching a man who had plain passed the point

170

where he cared to be sensible. Brautigan had felt it in himself once or twice, a recklessness brought on at last by heavy doses of self-restraint.

By sheer strength he bulled Briscoe across the floor and away from confrontation. When he looked back, he saw that Frazier had not moved, but that Cora Dawson had her arm around his waist, where it seemed to be doing some good.

The black woman, Effie, passed him, hurrying. In the next minute, she and Cora were laughing and hugging each other, a reunion.

But Briscoe saw only Frazier. "Nigger like that ought to be taken out and horsewhipped," he said.

"Doc, don't you be the one to try."

"Why the hell not?"

Brautigan thought for a moment of the several answers that applied and offered none of these. "Go help the little ones," he said.

Briscoe, who loved children, chewed his mustache for a moment, but finally went.

Two minutes later the first rock of the morning had their attention. It came through a window already broken and hit a little black girl on the knee, knocking her down. She screamed. As Brautigan ran for the door, he saw Peter McKenzie—where had he come from?—running for the child.

Sergeants Prendergast and O'Neill had already slammed the heavy oak bar in place behind the door. Glancing quickly about, Brautigan saw that all over the armory metropolitans were taking up the defensive positions he had assigned the night before.

It was last night's pattern all over again. Volleys of rocks and other missiles slamming against the Mulberry Street side of the building. Ragged volleys, accompanied by jeers, catcalls, general obscenities. They had suspect parentage. They had depraved sexual habits. Above all, they were nigger-lovers. The difference last night had been the three abortive attempts to reach Willie. Then the besiegers had shown their fury: a dozen wounded (including the supervisor), one police sergeant dead.

171

Brautigan took Prendergast's place at the door so that he could squint through the peephole.

"Same as last night," Prendergast said.

O'Neill said, "Maybe not quite. Might be the hangover's dampened them some."

"Don't bet your poke on it," Brautigan said after a moment.

He turned the post back to them and cut across the armory floor toward the corner near his own office where the blacks had chosen to cluster. There were now over a hundred of them. This included Dawson's contingent, the orphanage contingent, as well as families and stray individuals who had been coming in since noon the day before. Mostly women and children, only a sprinkling of men. Struck by that, Brautigan queried Dawson.

Frazier, standing next to him, said, "Ask Willie Jones."

Dawson nodded. "Many of our young men are dead," he said. "Many others left their families knowing they could not protect them, hoping the police would." He paused, hesitant.

"He wants to know if you're going to protect us," Frazier said.

"I don't mean you personally, Chief Inspector," Dawson said. "Please believe I have no doubts along that line. I am inquiring as to official policy."

"He wants to know if we've been dumped overboard," Frazier said.

"Round about noon yesterday," Brautigan said, "Supervisor Benton sent runners to all precincts with orders that no black was to be turned away."

Dawson said, "I am relieved, sir."

But Frazier said, "What if that white trash out there mounts a charge?"

"Then I will try to beat it back," Brautigan said.

"They outnumber you almost three to one. What if they try to overwhelm you?"

"They can't without firearms."

"What if they get firearms?"

"From where?"

"I don't know from where. But suppose they do?"

172

Brautigan turned to Dawson. "I promise—"

Frazier would not let him finish. "There are twenty men in here with black skins who have more to lose than anybody if that mob comes crashing in. Will you let us help?"

"Why wouldn't I?"

"Will you give us rifles?"

Brautigan was taken aback. "Rifles?"

"Rifles," Frazier said, enunciating with great care. "A moderate supply of them is locked in your office. If that mob has rifles, will you hand them out to us, too?"

"Who gave you permission to go in my office?"

Frazier was silent.

"No, I won't give you rifles," Brautigan said. "Those are authorized to police only."

Frazier smiled.

Brautigan, flushing, said, "What need is there of rifles? Rifles mean killing. And I don't want to see any more of it, black or white."

"Obviously there is merit in that position, Richard," Dawson said.

Frazier's smile remained intact. "The position is this. The chief inspector don't want no rifle in no black man's hand no way. That's the position."

They held each other's stares. It was Brautigan's that shifted finally. "Reverend Dawson," he said, "we'll do our best for you. You know we will."

"Yes, Chief Inspector."

Frazier left.

"He's not easy, is he?" Brautigan said, watching after him.

"He's a proud man, Chief Inspector. You must not think because a man is black he has no right to pride."

And he left, too.

Brautigan felt like a juggler with an errant plate. He felt inept, as if something significant had taken place before his eyes, but that he had been blind to it. He had trod on sensitivities, that much was obvious. But he was damned if he knew exactly how. Rosie

173

would have known. If she had been there, he could have turned to her and asked her questions. Rosie had the quick wit, the imagination that enabled her to live in another's skin for a while, even a black man's. But not big, clumsy John Brautigan. He was adept only at breaking heads. He was still staring after Dawson when Prendergast appeared.

"Please to come with me," Prendergast said.

He went. O'Neill moved away from the peephole. "Say the word, Chief Inspector, and me and Tom will go out there and kick his arse."

Thus, Brautigan knew just about what to expect when he took O'Neill's place. Nor was he disappointed.

Michael looked both ill at ease and rebellious. It was a combination with which Brautigan had long familiarity. It went with pennies stolen from Nora's pocketbook. Or a neighbor's window broken. Or capture by a truant officer. It was the look of misbehavior passing as bravado.

"The one standing next to Michael, the one in the fancy suit, that's Campfield," O'Neill said. "He was the one speechifying at the docks yesterday morning."

"I know," Brautigan said.

And as he spoke, the man in the white suit produced a large white handkerchief and began to wave it. He walked forward. When he was about twenty-five yards away he stopped.

"A word with you, Chief Inspector," he called out.

As effortless as it had been outside the provost marshal's office, though a shade more peremptory, Brautigan thought. Well, no sense keeping a busy man waiting. He stepped away from the door and nodded to the sergeants. They shot the bar back. He opened the door and started out, the sergeants instantly in his wake. With a gesture he halted them. With another he turned them around and waited until they were once more at their posts. Alone, then, he crossed Mulberry Street to join Campfield and Michael, and with them formed a small cluster not far from Willie Jones's lamp post. The heat *was* having its way with Willie, Brautigan noted. Next he saw that Campfield wanted him to note it.

174

"White or black, sir, it makes no never mind," Campfield said. "Don't follow."

"We'll hang who we have to, whoever it is who stands between us and our justice."

Brautigan turned to Michael. "How are you, son?"

Michael glanced away.

"We want your niggers, Chief Inspector," Campfield said.

"Why?"

"That's our business," Michael said.

Brautigan looked at him. "Since when did you get so all-fired bloodthirsty?"

"Bloodthirsty's got nothing to do with it."

Brautigan shifted deliberately so that Willie's gently swaying, grotesquely grinning corpse could become their centerpiece.

"Oh God," Michael said. "How could you believe I'd ever have anything to do with that? They did it, the mob. I had nothing to do with that. And I wouldn't ever."

"Then why do you want the blacks?"

"To march them out of town," Campfield said. "I promise you we mean no bodily harm to them. Unless, of course, we have to take them by force. If we do, well, then, tempers are likely to heat. And if tempers heat . . ." He paused, glanced critically at the folds of his handkerchief, perceived the need for a minor correction, after which he could continue. "White or black, sir, it will make no never mind. I mean, sir, there are thirty lamp posts on Mulberry Street alone."

"And while he's hanging me, Michael, what will you be doing, may I ask?"

"He won't be hanging you," Michael said sullenly. "That's the whole point."

"What is? Explain it to me. I never was so nimble-witted as you."

"The point is that's why we're out here talking, parleying. So that you can be made to understand how serious this is. Nobody wants anybody to get hurt. Give us the niggers, and we'll march them away, and that'll be an end to it."

175

Brautigan shook his head. "The men, women, and children who have asked for police protection will be given police protection. Good day, gentlemen."

He had covered not more than a couple of yards when Campfield called out, "We now have rifles, Chief Inspector."

Brautigan stopped and turned. "You aim to kill us all, Mr. Rifleman?"

"The name is Campfield, sir."

"That what Tyrell has in mind for us? Massacre?"

"Once again, Chief Inspector, if there's to be a massacre, you will be responsible for it. All we want is your niggers. And all we want from them is to get out of town and not return. And I may add, sir, that I have no knowledge of any Tyrell. Michael, has there been a Mr. Tyrell in our company this morning?"

Brautigan smiled. Then the smile faded, and he turned to his son. "What would Nora Brautigan be thinking, knowing you're on the take for Tyrell's dirty dollar?"

Michael drew back his arm as if to swing. Brautigan stepped forward and shoved him into Campfield so hard both men went sprawling into the grime of Mulberry Street. Michael was on his feet instantly. Just as quickly, Brautigan grabbed him, bearhugging him to keep him helpless.

But then he said, "Michael, Michael, what are we up to?"

He felt the boy slump against his chest. He eased his hold but did not let go. It became a different kind of embrace. Without breaking it he moved out of Campfield's hearing. "What are we doing to each other?"

Michael tore loose from him, as if he would run, but then he did not. He took a deep breath. Brautigan saw that the angry red in his face was now only a mottling. When he spoke there was something of a tremor in his voice, but he kept it soft. "No more of this. You're going to have to let me go, Pop, for good and all. I don't say it's anybody's fault, but we do it all the time."

"Why, Michael? Why do we?"

"Maybe it's just I can't stop thinking you want me to be Joey?"

"Joey's dead. Do I want you to be dead?"

176

"Joey's alive."

"You keep him alive."

"If that's so it's because I can't help myself."

Brautigan felt suddenly defeated. It was as if weapons he had absolutely counted on were, in some incomprehensible way, rendered obsolete. His voice was a tired man's. "I don't know what to say to that, Michael."

By now Campfield—whose suit had gone from splendid to shabby and who had spent the past few minutes attacking blemishes with his handkerchief—was ready to face the world again. He stood erect.

"In thirty minutes, sir," he said matter of factly, "these streets will be rivers of blood."

His manner and voice were as unruffled as ever. It was as if being upended in squalor were no more than an occupational hazard, Brautigan decided—glad to have something to decide that was not rooted in Michael.

"Whose man are you, Mr. Campfield?" he asked. "Tyrell's? Or do we have General Lee to thank?"

Campfield ignored that. "And I promise you, sir, that the niggers will not bless you for your efforts in their behalf. Give them to us, and at least they will live."

Brautigan turned from him and went back to the armory.

The sergeants opened the door for him, both grinning. They had seen their adversaries in the mud.

"Wipe it off," Brautigan said. "You won't think it so funny when that crowd's all over us with carbines popping."

O'Neill turned to Prendergast. "Didn't I tell you?"

"That's what Sergeant O'Neill guessed you was parleying about," Prendergast said. "Sergeant O'Neill says to me that's a son of a bitch with rifles up his sleeve, meaning Campfield."

"Well, Sergeant O'Neill, let's see how fast you can get the men alerted. And armed. Prendergast, you find Doc Briscoe and tell him he's got to move his field hospital back into the gymnasium where it'll be out of the line of fire. Get going. In ten minutes I want you both reporting to me in my office."

177

They galloped off.

"O'Neill!"

The little man doubled back.

"When you distribute arms I want the blacks included."

In twenty years of serving under Brautigan, Sergeant Kevin O'Neill had never once been tempted to disobey an order, but now Brautigan could see protest ablaze in his eyes. It was a transgression against the natural order of things. And the revered Brautigan the source of it!

"Request to repeat the order," O'Neill said.

"You heard me, Sergeant. Arm the blacks and put them under Frazier's command."

"Who—"

"You know goddamn well who he is."

"The men won't—"

Brautigan took a step forward. It brought him very close to O'Neill. For a moment he stood looking down at him. "I'll break heads, Sergeant," he said. "You tell them that."

"Yes, sir."

"Move."

Brautigan got himself another cup of coffee and took it with him to his office. There he replayed the scene he had just played with Michael. Only he changed the lines. Michael's were inconsequential. His were sharp, quick. Arrows, each one struck unerringly. Michael was left quivering. Magical arrows. Through them shame entered and worked its way into the bloodstream; not poison but an antidote to poison. As a result—even now—Michael was making his way to the Mott Street door to beg his father's forgiveness.

That passed. Once again he replayed the scene, changing the lines. Once again Michael's miscarried, but this time Brautigan's were more temperate, wiser. As a result Michael understood about Joey, that it was only because Michael had been so extraordinary, so fussed over, and Joey so bypassed and therefore so in need. Of course, Michael said inevitably. How odd I never saw it before.

When that passed Brautigan felt a renewal of the hopelessness

178

that had attacked him earlier. Heavily, he recalled Michael's demand for freedom. And he was tempted, he told himself. But even as he did he knew it for nonsense. He would look for Michael tomorrow and try to fix it, whatever was wrong between them. And if he failed, then he would try again the next day. And the day after that.

A knock at the door.

"Come in," he said, expecting either or both of the sergeants. It was Frazier. He had a carbine in his hand with which he saluted Brautigan, touching the barrel to his forehead.

"I am grateful to you, Chief Inspector."

Brautigan looked at him and thought about hatred. He thought about it so hard that for a while he almost forgot the other man was in the room.

Frazier said, "Your sergeant was not delighted to comply with your order. I don't mean that as any particular criticism of him. It just makes me wonder, sir, what caused you to change your mind."

"I'm no abolitionist if that's what you're reckonin'."

"I did not mistake you for one."

"Damn it, I don't say the abolitionists are dead wrong either. I'm just not political, that's all. Got enough to do looking after my own potato patch."

"That was my impression."

"But slavery is . . . Never did see how you could make a case for folks owning other folks."

Frazier shrugged.

After a moment Brautigan tipped his chair back against the wall. "As for O'Neill," he said, "I suppose that improves some about the time one of your lot stops a bullet meant for one of ours."

"Yes," Frazier said, and the two men regarded each other—not with affection, but at least with some kind of understanding.

Shutting the door of Brautigan's office, Frazier found Cora waiting for him. She gave him a cup of coffee. Her eyes were on the

179

carbine, but she said nothing. He slung it over his shoulder and then put his arm around her, moving her back toward the gymnasium. Deliberately, she went heavy. She was not going to make it easy for him to part from her.

"My only hope is we've begun a baby," she said.

He smiled.

She stopped walking and made him stop. "You're going to be killed today. I know it. You know it, too. You're resigned to it."

"Am I?"

"And I hate you for it."

"Good. Then if it happens—"

She meant to do no more than stop the words, but her hand slammed against his mouth so hard it rocked his head back. He had to clutch at the cup to keep it from falling. Carefully, then, he put it on the ground. Both hands freed now, he placed them beneath her elbows and lifted her. Straight up, holding her there like the figurehead of a ship. Or like the emblem of his life for all the world to see. Heads craned throughout the armory. Lowering her, he settled her against his chest. He kissed her. When he stopped kissing her he held her against him again, and she tried to imagine him dead. She could not. He was too solid, too vital. But that, she knew, was a fraud. Solid, vital, splendid as a king, none of that made any difference to a bullet.

But Frazier was no longer looking at her. He was looking over her shoulder, and something in his face made her twist sharply. Randy was coming toward them. Or, rather a shopworn version of him. His clothes were soiled; the ruby-headed cane, gone; though he still wore his cravat (knot somehow intact), patches of black skin showed through the mosaic of rips and rents in his pantaloons. But most of all he was tired. It was in his face and in the set of his shoulders. By now, Cora knew the signs of a man driven to hoard his energy.

"Where's Willie?" he asked, when he had reached them. He spoke first to Frazier. But then he turned to Cora. "I been hunting everywheres. Can't find him nowheres."

Frazier's grin was horrible. "You can't?"

180

"Cora, tell him where Willie is. Better still, why don't you show him?"

For an instant Randy's eyes sparked to life. "Safe?"

"He's safe, all right," Frazier said. "Not a buckra in the world can touch him now."

The spark faded. Randy said, "Willie gone. Knew it all the time. How?"

"They hanged him," Frazier said. "They also cut his pecker off. The thing I'm not sure of is if they did that after he was dead."

Randy shut his eyes. He muttered something unintelligible, broken, but when he opened his eyes again they were savage. "Want to see him," he said.

Cora moved away from them. Almost instantly she was back. She reached up to Frazier, shook him, then kissed him hard.

"Your son will look like you," she said, harshly. "He'll be beautiful, just as you are. But he'll grow up hating guns. And *all* men who use them. I promise you that."

They watched after her as she fled. Until, from the Mott Street side, the cry went up: "By God, here they come!"

181

4

It took Michael twenty minutes to run from the armory to his rooming house on Greenwich Street, a distance he had never before covered in under half an hour. But that was the measure of his panic. His flight had been virtually concurrent with the first shot fired by that black savage charging from the Mott Street door. It might not have been. Which is to say he might not have been quite so frightened had the bullet gone astray. Instead it was a direct hit. And the man standing just behind him—so close that seconds earlier Michael had been forced to jab him with an elbow to get some room—took the bullet in his face and went down, screaming. He screamed for almost ten seconds, long enough for Michael to realize that the hot sticky stuff on the back of his own neck was blood. He dropped the rifle Campfield had just put in his hands. Twenty-five minutes later he was in his own bed, with the covers pulled up around his ears. Within another five minute span he was deeply (and safely) asleep—though prey to a series of highly colored dreams, in which people, with clownish faces (white daubed with red) wept without ceasing.

He awoke drenched. A moment passed before he recognized his

own room. To recognize it was to find it unbearable. He looked at the clock on the mantel. Half past twelve. How hungry he was. Downstairs to the kitchen in search of Mrs. Schneider. Gone. No kindly note for him (as was her habit) to lead him to a cache of nutrients, playfully hidden in one of the pantry shelves. No note, no Mrs. Schneider, no creature stirring. Three landings full of emptiness. To test the truth of this, he called her name aloud. No response. Then: "I hate you, John Brautigan." No response. He tried a few wide-ranging obscenities meant to shrivel the capitalist corrupters of American society from Astor through Blanchard with a sharp drop to the Jardines. No response to that either.

He found a cookie tin. Two very stale, very small wheat cookies. He ate them.

He went out into the street. Deserted. Through his soles the blazing cobblestones burned his feet, and he danced from one to the other until he found an oasis under the awning of Rosenburg's Furniture Store. Across the street a scavenging pig suddenly appeared in the narrow alley between the warehouses of the Roanoke Tobacco Company and Amberson's Fine Leathers—with something indeterminate dangling from its mouth. The pig saw Michael, decided he was a threat, reversed field, and scurried back the way he had come. Desultorily, Michael followed, for no reason other than that it was the only movement on the landscape.

And, in fact, it was the pig that led him, five blocks later, to the corner of Catherine and Ann streets. Not that this was a corner new to him. Far from it. It was a corner grown quite familiar to him over the past year since it was occupied by Brooks Brothers, clothiers to the fashionable and Michael's place of business. A stock boy to begin with, he was now one of the establishment's five haberdashery clerks, by far the youngest. This was testimony to how well he was regarded by the store's proprietors.

Michael liked it at Brooks Brothers. Something about being surrounded by all those expensive clothes was soothing to him. He liked touching them. He liked wearing them—and, on occasion, he was asked to for the benefit of this or that truly significant customer. Moreover he was beginning to discover, preceded in

183

this by his employers, that he was a natural salesman. There were days when Michael dreamed he'd like to own a store like Brooks Brothers. On the other hand, there were days when he regarded that as criminally bourgeois. Between these extremes Michael did a good deal of wavering. But there were also days when he fancied himself a political leader, Tyrell's stripe. Or an actor. Or a firebrand radical, leading his oppressed brothers to freedom. Or the missing heir to wealth beyond avarice, identified as such by a discreet strawberry mark, and allowed to accede to lands, titles, and assorted prerogatives, while charged with no other task than spending. This was his favorite daydream.

The crowd at Catherine and Ann was already immense when Michael got there in the wake of the pig; almost twice the size of the mob that had besieged the armory. Its members were in the process of ripping away the iron grills and shutters that had been carefully erected to keep them out. Half were down. The remaining half would not last long.

It was, as usual, a drunken mob. Michael looked for people he knew. Almost immediately he spotted Grissom, a fellow clerk. Grissom was the clerk ranked just above Michael, in age as well as seniority. He was a tall, ginger-haired young man whose intelligent face was marred by a bright cluster of pimples that seemed to make bimonthly trips from one side of his jaw to the other. It was rumored that Grissom (Cyrus) was distantly related to the store's founders, but no one that Michael knew could pinpoint the particulars. In Michael's view Grissom was the source of the rumors. Between Michael and Grissom, there was little love lost. Michael thought Grissom an imitation Englishman with supercilious manners and an ambitious, driving nature. Grissom thought Michael a first-generation oaf with cloddish manners and an ambitious, driving nature. Each, on sight, was wont to experience a tingling awareness of the other as *the* obstacle in the path of promotion and fulfillment.

But that was the way they felt on an ordinary day. On this extraordinary day, with the crowd milling, pushing, shoving, grunting, swearing, and clearly getting ready for some enthusias-

184

tic looting—with two of the large plate glass windows on Ann Street already smashed and paving stones being hurled at their Catherine Street counterparts—Michael and Grissom were glad to see each other, experienced a surprising flush of solidarity.

"Wonder if our employers are anywhere around," Grissom said, eyeing the surrounding buildings. "If they are, wonder if they like the fashion show." He indicated a row of rock throwers on the Catherine Street side—ten of them, all wearing Brooks Brothers beavers, appropriated from the Ann Street window.

"Let's go," Michael said.

"Where?"

"In the back way before they pick everything clean."

Grissom hesitated. "I say, Brautigan, it can't be you have thievery in mind."

"I ain't got a thing in mind. You coming?"

"I'll rue it tomorrow," Grissom said but hesitated no longer.

Through the Catherine Street entrance. Clattering up the long, rickety flight of wooden stairs that took them, breathless, to the upper floor. Plunging into the gloom of the back corridor (since no one had flared the lamps); past the pattern room, with its naked male mannequins, past the B & B room (buttons and bows) and onto the vast, marbled selling floor, with its stately columns, its files-on-parade tables piled high with merchandise—woolens, linens, cottons, every kind of fabric provided it was pricey and difficult to come by.

Hard as they had run, they were too late to be among the first. Drunks were everywhere, swarming, men and women. As were the signs of the havoc they had already wrought. Mannequins had been toppled, stripped; in some cases, mutilated. Mirrors broken. Pictures desecrated. The noise level was indescribable, and, row on row, covering the front staircase, was the by now familiar New York City sight: antlike processions of looters, bearing away whatever was not nailed down.

"You know what I'd like to do?" Michael asked.

"I suspect something outrageous."

"See the sanctum sanctorum."

185

"On your own then," Grissom said and began moving away.

Michael grabbed his arm. "Have you ever seen it?"

"Of course."

"Liar."

"Good day to you, young Brautigan. I won't say it's been an unmixed delight."

"Under what circumstances? Nobody ever gets invited there who isn't worth at least a million, and you know damn well that's true."

Grissom smirked. "You mean nobody who isn't a relative."

"Humbug."

Grissom shrugged.

"All right," Michael said, "then I'll go alone."

"Excellent decision."

He started off, but almost at once bumped into a very fat old woman whose arms were heaped high with summer broadcloth. Companionably, she grinned at them both. "Excuse me, young sirs. Didn't mean to knock you about." Extricating a piece of ruffled shirting from her broadcloth pile, she offered it to Michael. "Yours for a dollar and cheap at twice the price. And won't you look the toff, my beauty."

Before he could answer they heard a scream from outside, and all three hurried to one of the Catherine Street windows. Two policemen were being beaten unmercifully. As they watched one of them went down and was immediately lost under a human avalanche. But the other somehow managed to break free. Pursuers strung out behind him, he rounded the corner and scurried down Ann Street. At first it seemed he might be recaptured, but he was young and sober. And after fifty yards he was outdistancing them.

"That's it," the old lady said. "If the police ain't already on their way they certain sure will be when that bluecoat reaches home base." Squinting at Michael. "Half a dollar, and Edwin Booth himself won't be the match of you."

Michael shoved past her roughly. She spat at him. He took a threatening step, and she scooted off with surprising speed.

186

He turned to Grissom. "Last chance."

"I told you. I've seen it."

"Yes, only you were lying."

Grissom grinned. "Have you forgotten—the bluecoats are coming."

Michael was not sure himself why it was so important that Grissom not desert, but it was. Part of it, he knew, was the nagging worry—evidence existed—that Grissom was the better strategist. And that if he chose defection it would turn out to be sound tactics. Michael was torn. The risk gave him pause. And yet he really longed to see the room. He had caught tantalizing glimpses of it. Rich, sleek men had gone in there, as if to some elite club. He had heard their laughter, the sounds of jovial conversation. Rich men's laughter, rich men's talk, redolent of power and influence. He had imagined the schemes they'd hatched to become even more powerful. Never again would he have so marvelous an opportunity to see this legendary room. On the other hand, old Martin Demeret, chief habadashery clerk, was rumored to be retiring. . . .

"You'll regret it," Michael called to Grissom, who was already ten feet away and moving briskly.

Without turning Grissom waved a negligent hand.

Reluctantly, Michael started after him. Went a few feet, stopped. An image of Tyrell had popped into his mind. Would Tyrell let anything on earth stop him if he had a yearning as sharp as Michael's? He would not. And had not Tyrell perceived in Michael the qualities of a coming man? He had. Michael fought anxiety to a standstill. Squared his shoulders. Found the corridor he had just left and continued along it until he came to the red leather door with a huge golden knob. He ran his fingers caressingly over the tiny gold lettering that said, Private—and then turned the knob.

Locked. And yet it never had been before. It was a matter of pride with the proprietors—some said arrogance—that Brooks Brothers people required only instructions to keep them from straying. But no matter how he worked the knob the door would

187

not budge. And then, with a bitter pang of disappointment, he realized that special measures had been taken against the mob. He had already turned away when Grissom appeared, an ax slung carelessly over his shoulder.

"I say, old man, would something like this come in handy?"

Michael took it from him, but did not swing it. "What made you come back?"

"The devil in me, if you must know. The same black devil that's going to plague me all my life and keep me from getting as far as I should."

Three blows, and the door splintered. Grissom started through, but Michael grabbed his arm.

"Admit it. You've never been in here."

"Unhand me, old bean."

"Admit it, or you don't get by."

"Oh well, under *those* circumstances . . ." Bowing. "Sir, you have me dead to rights."

"Humbugger," Michael said, and they went through as if in harness.

The room was huge. Dominated by red velvet, red and black leather, and black walnut, it reeked with masculinity. The fireplace was magnificent—over it, an ample sideboard glittering with cut glass and decanters of whisky, brandy, Holland gin, and other more exotic distillations. (Grissom helped himself to the brandy.) Steel engravings hung on the walls; landscapes, seascapes, hunting scenes, racing scenes, boxing scenes, and one opulent pink-fleshed nude. From brackets near each window were suspended brass cages, though the birds that should have occupied these were gone. Everywhere potted plants and vases (now empty) added splashes of color to the room while reminding that the Brooks brothers were partial to canaries and flowers. Gleaming porcelain cuspidors, decorated with sprays of roses, were scattered around on the carpeted floor. Two red leather sofas—each with its complement of overstuffed chairs—and a giant grand piano completed the furnishing.

For Michael the impact was overwhelming. What must it be like

188

to own a room like this? How confident it must make a man feel. How sure of his place. You would always know the right thing to say if you owned a room like this. You would always know the right way to order in an expensive restaurant and the right fork to use. And, of course, you would always have the right friends and the right women. You would never see another cockroach as long as you lived. And, God, the clothes you would have.

The prospect of all this splendor took Michael's breath away. He could not move a step beyond the three that had brought him across the threshhold. He could not make himself sit down in one of the leather chairs though he yearned to do so. He became conscious of Grissom grinning at him. Furious, he turned toward him, but by that time the grin had disappeared and its owner had moved to the piano. Grissom began to play, taking Michael by surprise. He played with unmistakable authority, yet he had never even mentioned that he was musical. Nor was the music anything likely to be heard in the Broadway halls and theatres. It was high-toned, fancy—the kind of music toffs in evening dress went to hear.

Grissom, who had been watching Michael, shook his head. "You are a damn fool, young Brautigan. By heaven, you are." And in his face there was . . . ferocity. The only word for it. So uncharacteristic it startled Michael.

"What do you mean? What are you talking about?"

Grissom crashed some chords, then stopped playing abruptly. He stood up. "There you are in a snit because you can't play the bloody piano. Full of resentment, aren't you, you silly bastard? What difference does the bloody piano make to anything? And what difference does it make that I'm smarter than you are, better educated, and probably more deserving in general? I'll tell you what difference it makes. None. Because the fact is I'm homely. I've a skinny neck. And pimples on my face, sweet Jesus. And you're a goddam Adonis. Which is why starting next Monday our esteemed brothers Brooks are putting you, not me, in charge of the bloody department."

Michael stared at him. "How do you know?"

189

"I know, that's all. Oh for God's sake, Marty Demeret told me."

Michael managed to get himself to one of the chairs. He sank into it.

"Bloody, silly snot," Grissom said and walked out, slamming the remnant of a door behind him.

Michael tried to come to terms with what he had just heard. Could it actually be true? If it were true, it could mean . . . Oh, if only it were true, it would mean . . . what? Why, at least a first step up. More money. Enough to find new lodgings? Certainly enough for that. New clothes? Yes, yes, of course.

He found himself unable to sit still. He crossed to the sideboard, examined the labels on the bottles. The names were marvelous, the bottles splendid-looking. Fit for a celebrant. For a moment he was tempted. He lifted a bottle of French champagne, but then, superstitiously, thrust it back. That would be an indulgence. And who could be certain it would not disturb some precarious alliance of favorable fates. Besides, he was drunk enough already on Grissom's news. He wished nothing to dull the sensation. And it was not merely the money, or even the implications in terms of his career. It was a sign, a symbol. It meant a change in what life had in store for him. He was certain of that. So certain, that all the biliousness in him, the niggardliness, the wintriness of outlook was replaced with warmth and love for everyone. His father. My God, wouldn't John Brautigan be surprised. Wouldn't he be delighted.

He ran from the room like a sprinter. But it was only a yard or two before the sound of raised voices reached him. He kept going. When he turned the corner, he saw that the next corridor was jammed. Police. On the attack. Swinging locust sticks remorselessly. Swarms of them. People screaming, fleeing, falling. The awful thud of wood connecting solidly with bone.

Michael was terrified. He saw a window. Opening to where? He looked. Thank God, a fire escape. Below it a relatively short drop into the back alley. Deliverance. Out the window onto the fire escape, then skittering down the ladder to the last rung. For a moment he hung from that by his hands, preparing himself for the

190

drop—ten feet, no more. Child's play. Particularly for the newly designated chief of Brooks Brothers haberdashery who was ten feet tall himself.

He saw the metropolitans burst into the alley just as he let go; no way to stop himself. He yelled a warning. It was misunderstood. He landed on top of one of them and was immediately shot by the other. He managed to get to his knees. Wildly, with eyes already opaqued and useless, he looked about in disbelief and then fell back into the dirt and debris of the alley, dead before he stopped moving.

5

From Stephen Jardine's diary. Tuesday, July 4:

And so Independence Day, 1863, dies of its wounds. Such an Independence Day as even our bleakest forefathers . . .

The Battle of Bunker Hill . . . all glory . . . all idealism.

The Battle for Willie Jones's corpse . . . all horror.

There he hung, Willie, only seemingly at the end of a rope. Actually, it was a chain. A chaotic chain. A wartime thing composed of self-evident truths along which opposing armies move—to arrive at a place of nightmare.

I doubt the above makes any sense at all.

I am too weary to think sense, how can I write sense?

Reports keep coming in of the carnage at the armory. Certain it is that the "howling devils" were put to rout—guns and all, but details are worrisomely sketchy.

I know that John was there. And Michael—on the other side!

And Peter, too.

I hope all three of them are safe and . . .

Oh, you humbug!

She said to me, "Stephen, if you have something on your mind I would be glad to hear it."

And of course there was something in the way she . . . And so of course the words I spoke had no reference to anything I could possibly have meant: "If I had something to say I would not wait for permission."

She looked at me. Reflexively, my own glance moved away. I ordered it back. Hers took flight.

But that's the way it is with us these days. Our glances have lives of their own, and when they meet it's always by accident. How strange we are. I think of us as in a horror story. Fantasy figures, gifted . . . scratch that . . . cursed with a Poe-like ability to see the future. And what do we see? Why, sir, we see ravens.

Ugh!

Near midnight now; and things have quieted at last. The mobocracy has gone to its lair, fatigued. Why not? They have been at us since 5:00 A.M.

All day armed crowds marched the city, setting as much of it as they could to the torch—rich man's, poor man's, no man's goods were sacrosanct. All day fire bells, alarm after alarm, peeled distress calls, each conflagration drawing its own vast throng to revel in the joy of devastation.

The mayor has issued a proclamation—go home, go home, obey our laws, etc., etc. So has the governor, from afar. So has Tyrell, for that matter, who is now, no doubt, beginning to worry about his various vested interests. (He is Boss of nothing if there is nothing to Boss.) So has the clergy, from an array of pulpits. But the mobocracy responds to religious thunderation with something less than awe, I fear. More receptive, I fear, to . . .

Just arrived. A wire from Secretary Stanton to the mayor, a copy of which was sent by runners to all city newspapers: "Sir, three regiments are under orders to march to New York. The retreat of

193

Lee has become a panic, with his army broken and much heavier loss of killed and wounded than was supposed. This will relieve a large force for the restoring of order in New York."

So the soldier boys are coming.

But for how many of us will they arrive too late?

What is the effect of soldier boys on ravens?

Wednesday
July
5,
1863

"Yes," Margaret said. "Aunt Singleton is the only one I know who won't think the riots all bad."

But her smile had strain in it, Rosie thought. It was the same strain she noted in Stephen's face. The sign of a quarrel? No, the sign of a quarrel suppressed, one that should have been allowed its head in the hope of clearing the air. Margaret had her Blanchards-can-cope look, Rosie thought. Stephen's carriage was self-consciously erect, his eyes miserable.

Gently, Margaret shook her. "Your John will not be pleased. He thought he had you safely shelved."

"He is not my John. Nor am I his Rosie, for him to tell me where to go and where not to."

Margaret studied her. "They have quarreled," she said to Stephen. "Did you know that?"

"Yes."

"Why didn't you tell me?" But she did not wait for him to answer. She turned back to Rosie. "Lucky for you I'm in a hurry now, but be prepared for an inquisition." Blanchardy-brittle, and she knows it, Rosie thought, as Margaret kissed her and hurried into the carriage. No backward glance for Stephen.

"She's trying to commandeer a special ferry for the orphanage children, get them over to Blackwell's Island," Stephen said, not meeting Rosie's eyes. He took her bag, carried it into the house and upstairs to her room. When he came back down, however, she saw that his mental set had shifted. Now he had something other than Margaret on his mind; he had Rosie.

"Chuck him out," he said, "and you risk losing the best man ever likely to come your way."

She found herself with her face against his waistcoat. It was some few minutes before she could stop crying, after which she shoved him from her.

"Chuck him out indeed," she said, returning his handkerchief to him. "Is that what he told you? Arm-weary from trying to reel him in is more like it."

"He adores you, Rosie."

"For all the good it does either of us," she said. Then, having

Dourly, Rosie looked out the window of the hack. What she saw there did not improve her mood. Nor did listening to the driver. From the ferry north—nonstop over ten battle-scarred Broadway miles—he had regaled her with an ode to his own bravery. Only the lion-hearted, he insisted, would dare make such a journey. That was all right. Rosie did not mind a bit of puffery in behalf of a tip. It was when he shifted from his bravery to her foolishness that she began to grow vexed. Finally, she ordered him to hold his tongue. He obeyed. During the rest of the trip throug the deserted streets, the only sound was produced by the th middle-aged mare wearily clip-clopping over the cobblestone

Having paid the driver (a fattish tip after all), she was on point of dismissing him when Margaret appeared at the do number fourteen. "I need him, Rosie," she called out.

Rosie held the driver in place, and a moment later Margar Stephen were at her side. "How far along is young Stephen being spoiled rotten?" Margaret asked.

"His aunt is at work on it."

squared her shoulders and taken a restorative breath, she said, "Go on about your business. Leave the two of us to sort it out, or not sort it out if that is what it must come to."

He hesitated.

"It *is* between the two of us, Stephen."

"Of course it is. And a matched pair for mulishness if ever there was one. It's just that I'm not sure I like leaving you here alone, the city being what it is right now."

"The city is the city and never saw the day when Rosie Shannon needed a chaperone to make it mind its manners."

He continued to show signs of unwillingness. With her parasol she jabbed purposefully at his midriff, backing him up.

"All right, but not a single step out of this house do you dare. Is that understood?"

"Yes, sir."

"And lock all the doors."

"Certainly, sir."

"I'm still not . . ."

"Good-bye, Stephen."

Reluctantly he made preparations.

"Stephen . . ."

He stopped, and she ran to him, took his hands and squeezed them. "Maybe he has managed to fluster her a little," she said, "but no more than that. I mean that's the worst of it. And she will come to her senses, I promise you. She goes a bit giddy sometimes . . . like me . . . but the fact is she has the best head on her shoulders of anyone I know."

His face had stiffened. But then—smile twisting as he tried for her sake to improve its quality—he said, "Yes, of course." She knew it was the best he could do. He kissed her and left.

Was there truly a threat, she asked herself as she went about the house dutifully locking doors. Until today she had not believed in it. She had grown used to thinking of them as a couple without bumps or pits; that is, as having a surface so smooth nothing dangerous could grab hold of it to pry them apart. Had she underestimated Peter Mackenzie? She felt a surge of anger di-

199

rected at Margaret. Stephen was to Peter as gold to gilt. What kind of Blanchardy nonsense was she up to?

Masculine gold having been suggested, she thought then of her own nugget. *Fool's* gold, she decided vexatiously. Could anything be more provoking than this persistent refusal of his to act in his own best interests? Or hers, for that matter. Out of some ill-conceived notion of obligation. Or duty. Or whatever male-oriented piece of high-falutinism he had in mind. *Blast* obligation. Now was now. And anyone who didn't know that knew little worth knowing. Her hands curled into fists. They had done so regularly since her parting yesterday with the nonpareil of the metropolitans. This time she broke a nail. That seemed to her so eminently unfair she almost burst into tears again. Fighting them back, she clumped up the stairs.

She went to her room but was disinclined to rest, though she had been up most of the previous night. The room was hot, the bed uninviting. Only one night away, and it all felt strange to her; not strange in the sense that it was unfamiliar, but in the sense that it seemed not to fit. Rosie Shannon's room and things, true enough, but not *hers* somehow.

Which was certainly an absurd way to feel about items such as the sampler her mother had given her on her sixth birthday. And the stuffed elephant (with "never forget me" embroidered along its purple trunk) that John had bought her the first time they had walked out together (to Barnum's Museum). And the red leather memory book on her bureau. And the photograph next to it of her parents, and the one of Michael looking arrogant (but not really unlovable) in the mustache he had struggled so mightily with last year. And . . . oh, humbug! It was her mood, of course, and nothing at all to do with the room.

Who did he think he was, the big ox? She was a woman grown, thank you very much, and used to making her own decisions. How dare he behave toward her as if she were a child to be protected against herself. The sheer effrontery of this brought her to her feet and set her roaming restlessly.

As an aid to banishing Brautigan—(figurative exile was the least

200

he deserved)—she tried to recall another occasion on which she had been alone in the house. She could not. Usually when the Jardines were out there was young Stephen's noise to contend with, or the servants, but today nothing more than the thud of her own footsteps. These were oddly disturbing, however; heavier than they should be, it suddenly seemed to her; ominous.

Ominous? Ominous indeed! Ominous, my girl, in the middle of a sun-swept July afternoon? The next thing you know you'll be cringing before your own shadow and dropping to your knees and crossing yourself like the old ladies at St. Agatha's before venturing Broadway at the height of traffic. Rosie Shannon, what's got into you?

And then, just as she reached the top of the stairs leading from the kitchen, she heard the sound of breaking glass. She came to an abrupt halt. She saw a thick boot smashing in one of the large bay windows in front. She wanted to run; she could not. It was as if she were a figure in a nightmare, frozen, immobilized by an implacable dreamer. A lifetime passed. At last the dreamer relented, and she broke free; scrambled up the stairs. She reached the first landing before she heard the sounds of pursuit. Which room? She lost two or three seconds trying to decide before electing her own at the far end of the corridor. She locked the door, leaned against it, listened—and heard her name called!

"Hey, Rosie. Come on now, Rosie. Nobody wants to hurt you."

Pat Murphy, unmistakably. That high-pitched voice, burbling, as if the vocal chords were drawn through a jug of mush. In a moment she became certain he was not alone. Bridget and Dennis were with him. The family circle intact.

Reassurance from them, too. "We'd never harm a hair of your pretty head, Rosie," Dennis said. Titters. Drunken ones. "Hey, lass, speak up. Just answer a question or two, and we'll leave you in peace."

She said nothing.

Bridget: "We got a message for you from the chief inspector. Saints, lass, we come all this way to give you this urgent message, and here's our bloody thanks."

201

Pat: "Come on, ma. Let's get for home. She don't want no news from the chief inspector. Leastaways through us. Lace curtain she is now. Looks down her nose at her school chums."

Bridget: "You hear that, Rosie? You want us to go back to the old neighborhood and tell everybody there you think you're too good for them now?"

And then Pat screamed. "Bitch, where are you?"

She bit her lip.

"We'll find you, bitch. You know we'll find you, and when we do we'll make you sorry."

The sound of footsteps scurrying. Following this the sound of bodies hurtling against the door of young Stephen's room, two removed from hers.

It shocked her. She ran to the window to see if she dared escape that way. She ran quietly as she could, but Bridget heard her.

"There, Paddy. That one."

Bodies slamming into her door. It swung back against the wall, broken. Three grinning faces. Her own stiff with fright.

"Jardine," Bridget spoke from the threshhold.

But the two men came into the room and grabbed her. Pat twisted her arm up high, making her groan, causing his father to giggle.

Bridget, still from the threshhold: "Where is he?"

"I don't know. I just got back to the city an hour ago."

"Liar. Lying bitch," Pat said.

"Look. On the bed. There's my bag. I haven't even unpacked yet."

They looked, and for a moment Rosie thought she had earned a reprieve. Because it was clear they believed her. She even felt Dennis's grip slacken a bit.

But not Pat's.

Something malevolent came into his face. An idea formless the moment before now took shape, and he turned to his mother. "She's lying." He said the words slowly, holding her stare, inviting her to become coconspirator. When he saw that she would, he said, "But leave her to us. We'll get the truth out of her."

202

"I'm not—"

Without even looking at her he backhanded her across the face. "Shut your gob. I'll tell you when you're allowed to speak. By God, if you'd spoken when you were asked to, you wouldn't be in the trouble you're in now."

"You better not hurt me, Pat Murphy."

"Shut your gob, I said."

"Because if you do . . ."

She felt Dennis's grasp slacken further. "She means Brautigan," he said, and Rosie was glad to hear the anxiety in his voice.

"Brautigan be damned," Pat said. "We got orders from Tyrell. What's Brautigan against Tyrell?"

Bridget looked at her husband scornfully. "What's Brautigan against Tyrell?"

"But I don't—"

"Liar," he said again.

This time instead of hitting her he put his hand in her bodice and jerked down until he tore it. She tried to twist away, but now Dennis's grip on her was tight again. She could not get free of him. Pat kept tearing until the tops of her gown and chemise were in shreds. She was naked to the waist. She heard Dennis gasp, felt the heat of his breath. All three were staring at her. Her stomach turned. She thought she might be going to vomit.

Pat cupped a breast in each hand. "Saints, you ever see anything so pretty?"

Dennis giggled shakily.

Bridget went to the window, posting herself there as sentry, back to the room.

Rosie started to cry, hating herself for it. She wanted to be able to stare straight into Pat's eyes. She wanted to be arrogant, to spit in his face. She could not. She was too frightened.

His hand reached into her clothes again. She pulled away sharply, so sharply she caught Dennis by surprise. For a moment she was actually free. She ran for the door and might have made it through except that the remnants of her gown tripped her. She fell hard. Pat was on her instantly. Under the pretense that he was

203

trying to recapture her his hands were all over her. Dennis joined the game. She kicked and scratched and fought to get free, but they merely played with her. She screamed as loudly as she could. Pat's blow knocked her senseless.

When she came to, she was on her bed tied to its posts with an assortment of things pulled from her bureau, spreadeagled and naked. She had no idea of how long she'd been out but thought it could not have been long. Dennis and Pat stood together at the foot of the bed, grinning at her.

She turned from them, toward the sentry still at her post, and as she did felt the horror of fingers on her ankle. She strained away from the touch. "Bridget Murphy, are you not going to stop them?"

"From what? They ain't hurting you."

The weight of one of them was on the bed. She jerked her head around and saw Pat—on his knees, trousers down. She had thought her throat too dry for screaming; it was not.

Bridget said, "Paddy, mind what you're doing now. Fun's fun, lad, but . . ."

Pat grunted something unintelligible. Rosie, eyes shut, felt his weight settle on her. She felt his fingers probing. If only she could faint. Oh God, was that too much to ask?

Bridget: "Get off her. Now!"

Pat: "What? What?"

Rosie opened her eyes as Bridget, with both hands in her son's hair, pulled him off. Relief swept over her, and in that first moment of enormous gratitude she thought to herself: I knew she would not let them. No woman could so betray another.

But then Bridget said, "Brautigan."

Dennis scrunched himself up against the wall.

Blinking, Pat groped at his pants. Bridget was already at the bedroom door, Dennis half a step behind. Rosie heard the front door open. And so did the Murphys; they stopped, frozen.

"Is there a back stairs?" Bridget asked Rosie.

Rosie heard the hysteria in her laugh.

"He'll kill us," Bridget said.

"How I hope he does."

"If he does he's a murderer. You want your man to be a murderer?"

"John, I'm up here. Hurry before they get away."

The Murphys backed from the door to the far corner of the room, huddling near the window where Bridget had been sentry. Silently, as if all four were in the grip of suspended time, they stared at each other while Brautigan pounded up the stairs.

"I'm all right," Rosie said the instant he appeared in the doorway.

But his face went white anyway.

Pat shrieked. "You harm us and you'll have Tyrell to reckon with. He—"

Before he finished Brautigan had reached him, fingers throttling.

Dennis disappeared through the door. But Bridget was on Brautigan's back flailing at him, screeching. He paid no attention to her.

Rosie watched avidly. Exulting. She wanted Pat in agony. She wanted him dead. And then, quite suddenly, she didn't. "John, let him go. Come to me. I need you."

He swept Bridget off him, threw Pat after her so that he landed only inches away, rag dolls both of them. Bridget took Pat's head and cradled it to her thin bosom while he sobbed.

Brautigan untied Rosie. He wrapped her in the bedspread and held her against him in much the same way Bridget was holding Pat. Rosie wept. And so, for a moment, oddly unaware of each other, they were, in effect, bookends—Brautigan comforting Rosie, Bridget her son.

"You're to leave the city," Brautigan said. "The three of you. I want you gone by nightfall, and I don't ever want to smell the stink of you again."

Bridget got up and pulled Pat to his feet. He was still sobbing when they exited.

Rosie could not stop touching his face. "I was so frightened, John."

His arms tightened about her.

205

"How did you know I'd be here?".

"I didn't. I came to warn Stephen."

"You knew they were after Stephen? How?"

"The Boss does that every so often. Sometimes Stephen, sometimes me, whoever's worrying him at a particular time. It always means he's getting rattled." He paused. "Mary Haines sent me a message," he said, the tips of his ears coloring at the mention of so infamous a name. "She watches over Stephen a bit you know."

She enveloped herself in his solid presence. How good it felt to be there, to be lost in him. How safe. How much the harbor he was. And always had been. Her sweet, gentle lover. Her protector and her lover. Her mentor and her lover. And, ah, God, she'd die for him. She sought words to tell him some of this and could not find them. She settled for saying his name and wrapping him in her own vise, hard, trying to hurt him, so that he might understand, once and for all, that she never intended to let him go.

206

2

Colonel Bunce sat watching General Macklin. He was dismayed. Seldom during the past quarter century had he thought of the general as anything but the most vigorous of men. The idea of a healthy Macklin was as fixed in Bunce's mind as, say, the idea of a feckless enlisted man. Now, however, the general's face was pale, his mouth tremulous, his hands folded . . . evocatively, oh, much too evocatively . . . over the blanket, and he looked exhausted. He looked frail.

Bunce wanted to dampen the general's dry mouth, but when he moved to do it, Macklin's eyes flew open.

"Didn't mean to startle you, sir," Bunce said hurriedly.

"Never startled," the general said after two or three breaths had calmed him. He motioned Bunce to lean closer. "Terrible place," he said. "Terrible. Military hospitals always are."

On the verge of correcting him, Bunce caught himself. He smiled acquiescence, but the general was watching him and suddenly his eyes cleared. "Damn fool Bunce," he said. "Thinks I'm senile. Thinks I don't know I'm in the goddam Metropolitan Hospital for civilian arseholes. Bunce, remember when . . ."

Dating back to a period twenty years ago when the general had been commandant at West Point and Bunce his aide, the reminiscence was vividly salacious. And though largely untrue, it made Bunce blush. Grinning wickedly, the general patted his hand.

"You always were an old lady," he said.

"Yes, sir."

Macklin smiled. "But a brave old lady."

"Thank you, sir."

Unhurriedly, then, like the lowering of colors during retreat, the lids came down to cover the general's eyes.

Time passed. Bunce continued to sit, but his own lids had become an impossible weight. He kept drifting off. Once he caught himself just short of toppling from his chair. He, too, had had very little sleep the past two days, and he knew that in order to function properly, he would have to go home and catch up a bit. There were things to be done, many things to be done. And to whom but Bunce could the general pass the torch?

Bunce tiptoed out of the room.

Peter, who had seen him when he first entered the hospital, tried again to pretend he hadn't, but Bunce bore down on him.

"Mackenzie. I say there, Major Mackenzie, a word with you."

"What is it, Bunce? I'm busy."

"*Colonel* Bunce."

"*Colonel* Bunce, *Colonel* Bunce. Damn it to hell, man, we have a hospital full of people who need attention, and you waste my time playing soldier. What is it you want?"

"Proper accommodations for the general. In the last twenty years, General Macklin has shared his billet only with Mrs. Macklin, God rest her soul. Do I make myself understood?"

Peter felt warmth gathering under his collar. "We have here, sir, a hospital bursting at the seams. People have been getting killed and wounded for the last two days."

"I need hardly be informed of that, sir."

"Damn it, there *are* no private rooms."

"Create one."

A contest of stares. The force of conviction triumphed over

208

mere bad temper, and Peter's stare gave way. "Oh for God's sake, talk to Briscoe. He's in charge here. Why bother me with this nonsense?"

"Briscoe is not army, sir. And may I remind you, major, that you are."

Bunce folded his arms on his chest.

"Damn it, I'll do what's possible. Would have anyway without your bloody interference. For some inexplicable reason, I admire the old saber-rattler, believe it or not." He paused. "Aren't you going to ask for a prognosis?"

"I don't have to."

"No? You're a surgeon in addition to being a military genius?"

"He is dying."

Once more stares locked. But when Peter spoke this time, it was with a different kind of sharpness, the kind needed to mask the fact that something in Bunce's eyes had moved him.

"Yes," Peter said. "He's ready." He clamped his teeth on a longer speech, then shook his head. "Good day to you, sir. I *am* busy." But after two steps he halted. "You're not traveling these streets alone, are you?"

"Troopers are in short supply."

"Man, man, are you saying to me you are without military escort? Are you mad? 'Bloody Butcher Bunce' is being chalked on walls all over the city."

"They may write what they wish. When I fire into a mob to protect respectable lives and property, I do no more than a soldier's duty."

A brisk little bow, and he was into his exit while Peter called after him, "They can hardly be expected to share that view, Colonel."

Riding northward from Twenty-first Street and Second Avenue, Bunce saw no one. Street after street, however, testified to the primal mood of the past three days. Only the occasional structure remained unharmed. The rule was shattered windows. Torn awnings. Craterlike holes in building and pavement. And everywhere mutilation by fire, as if, repeatedly, the city's enemies had attempted its murder.

Bunce saw no one and yet felt watched. Still, when he darted a glance at a tenement roof, it was always empty. And when he turned his head sharply to look back at a storefront, or the entrance of a building or an intersection, all was deserted. Occasionally, he heard a door slam. Or a window open. Or a shout. Once he heard a lusty basso deliver a snatch of aria from, it seemed, a point no more than a dozen yards away, but when he whirled to see the source, he could do no better than locate it in the vicinity of a truncated horsecar, askew across its tracks.

The sudden clatter of hooves on cobblestones. To his surprise Bunce made out Peter Mackenzie approaching at breakneck pace. "They've surrounded your house," Peter said, reining in. "They've been there for hours. About fifty of them, according to my informant, hoping you'd be foolish enough to come by."

"Thank you, sir. It was kind of you to warn me. I want you to know I am not unappreciative."

"You're going anyway?"

"Well, being so close now . . ."

"You blockhead," Peter said, exploding. "You army mule. Don't you understand? The only reason they haven't burned your house to the ground is they're hoping to lure you there. They hate you. They want to kill you. How can I be plainer?"

"Good day to you, Major."

"Why are you doing this?"

Bunce smiled. It was an officer class smile—cool and professional. And endlessly exacerbating to amateur bosoms in a state of upheaval. "My dear Mackenzie, the point is we simply cannot allow the rabble to terrorize us. It would be a tactical error of immense proportions."

"Fifty to one, Bunce. Isn't that a proportion?"

"But they are dogs, and I am a soldier."

Hopelessly, Peter watched him go—pudgy, sweaty, yet holding himself like Galahad. Peter swore under his breath and followed him. Aware of this Bunce stopped and turned. He was about to

210

urge Peter to go back when the first rock flew by. That one missed. The next one hit Bunce on the shoulder and shook his balance. The third, a small boulder, unhorsed him. And the fusilade ended instantly.

None of the rocks had been aimed at Peter. The implication was clear. Peter could ride to safety. For a moment he wanted to very badly, but somehow he could not put this plan in action. Frozen, he watched silent figures—men, women, children—pour from the buildings on both sides of the street to gather around the fallen soldier. Fifty, sixty, perhaps more. No screams, no shouts, but it was their very silence that was terrifying. He forced himself to spur his horse forward. No one tried to stop him.

When he reached Bunce he was just getting to his feet, shakily. Peter helped him up. An ugly gash over his left temple marked where the third missile had grazed him. A hit more direct might have killed him. As Peter examined the wound, he looked into Bunce's eyes and saw they were not yet in focus.

Then from the bowels of the crowd he heard a voice he knew, "Leave him be, major."

A moment later he made out the particular Zouave remnants and the naked skull that signified ex-sergeant Evarts.

"He don't need no fixing up," Evarts said, breaking through to the front row.

Peter ignored him. Dabbing at the wound with his handkerchief, he got rid of the worst of the dirt. And now it was Bunce who pushed him away. And drew his sword at the same time.

"Disperse," he said. His voice cracked. Not out of fear, but because he was still in shock. Someone in the crowd laughed.

Wheeling, Peter said, "All right now, you've had your fun with him. Go home, and—"

"We ain't half had our fun with him," Evarts said. And this was echoed, one way or another, throughout the crowd. Again no loud voices. No obvious drunkenness. No chest thumping, or any of the other ritualistic acts of mob bravado. Instead a purposefulness that was unnerving. It was as if they knew precisely where their savagery would take them and were in no hurry to end the trip.

211

Peter said, "Evarts, I know who you are. And I warn you that if—"

He never finished. He felt himself drawn backwards. Many hands. Too many to struggle against. And as one part of the crowd sucked him in, another surged toward Bunce. He saw Bunce raise his saber and try to bring it down. He could not. It was ripped from him. Now the crowd was no longer quiet. At first an angry buzzing; then an eerie kind of keening; then a roar.

Bunce was engulfed. Fists smashed into him, feet. He was torn at. Thrown high into the air, caught once, then allowed to thud to the pavement. From time to time, he was lost entirely to Peter's view as the crowd moved up and down the street in swiftly changing configurations. By now Peter was certain Bunce must be dead but still they worried him, bone to a pack of dogs. Finally, they stopped. And were silent. And then abruptly parted so that Peter could see what had been accomplished by ten minutes of mob energy.

Bunce was naked, of clothes and most of his skin. Only a tuft or two of hair was left to him. He bled from fifty different wounds. Peter was certain every facial bone was fractured, that the rest of Bunce's body was in a similar state. And yet he was not dead. Peter dared not touch him for fear of causing agony, but he could see the chest moving. And he could hear the steady drone that came from deep in the throat and was like a kitten weeping. It went on that way for five more minutes, Peter longing for morphine. He knelt by Bunce, watched over him. There was nothing else he could do. And then at last the sound cut away in a penultimate gurgling breath. An instant later it was over.

Peter had not heard the crowd move off, but when he stood and turned it was gone. All but Evarts. Evarts was still there, leaning against the side of the building.

"You're not human," Peter said. "Human beings cannot do that to each other."

Evarts did not look up. In his hands he held Bunce's revolver, holstered. He was looking at it as if leather and metal formed a still life of unequaled beauty.

"Do you plan to use it on me?" Peter asked.

Evarts grinned.

"If you do hurry up and get it over with. I'm not afraid."

"I see you ain't," Evarts said.

Hiding his limp as best he could, Peter walked slowly but steadily to his horse, any minute expecting the bullet to slam into his back. It was an excruciating feeling. And yet he had not lied. He was not afraid. He thought mostly of the sky, that it was less starry than they had all grown used to during the past three days. There was now about it a touch of cumulus. Rain coming. And he thought, regretfully, of Margaret.

He was about to put his foot in the stirrups when it happened. It was like being clubbed. He was propelled forward so sharply that his head struck the horse's flank with stunning impact. He fell but did not quite lose consciousness. He knew the bullet was in his spine. Not much pain. Numbness creeping through him.

He opened his eyes and saw Evarts' boots. Then Evarts knelt to him as he had knelt to Bunce.

"Why?" Peter asked.

Evarts did not answer. He fired again, this time into Peter's brain.

3

As the first child—a little girl carrying an armless rag doll and clinging to Jemima Wilson's hand—stepped out of the armory, Stephen glanced at his timepiece. Five minutes to ten. The ferry was scheduled to leave for Blackwell's Island at eleven-thirty. A dozen blocks to the wharf. They should make it with ease. But if something unforeseen occurred, would Dennison, the ferryboat captain, wait? At the thought of Dennison, Stephen's temper threatened to heat up again, but he cooled it by persuading himself that whereas the negotiation period had been nervewracking, the conclusion had been successful enough. Dennison, muttering, had seemed to acknowledge a commitment.

The orphan's parade progressed, wending its way southeast along Grand Street. A squad of a dozen metropolitans marched at its head, rifles at ready, bayonets fixed. But as yet the crowds were unprepossessing. Stephen, anxious, wondered if they would grow more substantive at the pier. All he could do was hope not, hope that the lateness of the hour would keep them away.

He saw a four-year-old, a boy, straw-thin, fall and begin to cry.

Margaret saw him, too. She ran to pick him up, comforting him, and restored him to his place in the column.

Absorbing him, the column maintained its pace. Not brisk, of course, but steady. Fifty children ranging in age from two (these were carried by nurses) to ten. All sizes. All shades—from chrome yellow to ebony. Most of them carried bundles of clothing, poignantly light. Flanking the children on both sides were the nurses—Effie and Jemima up front, just behind the police guard. Margaret was toward the rear, not twenty feet from Stephen. She marched with that slight awkwardness he found so charming, long strides knocking her skirts into fine eddies and tangles as she went. But they had not spoken since the start of the journey. Nor, for that matter, had they spoken before, except for the austere greetings exchanged on first seeing each other at 200 Mulberry Street.

The note she had sent had efficiently outlined the operational details—the hiring of the ferry, the timetable agreed upon, the makeup of the escort, the arrangements for the reception of the children on arrival. All admirably businesslike. Only at the end was there a hint of anything personal and then because she had no choice:

"Most of this was done in cooperation with John Brautigan. But suddenly he is nowhere to be found, and I confess myself in need of a masculine bark. 'Tis the ferryboat master, a man named Dennison, I wish barked at. He has taken my money and now refuses to guarantee that he will wait for us. And I shudder at the thought of turning up at the pier with all those children and having to languish there while mobs form. Handling beasts like Dennison is something you have always been good at. Will you see to him for me?"

And so he had left the *Tribune* and headed for the waterfront. The ferryboat master, whose normal converse was in grunts—the occasional snarl thrown in to make a point—required considerable seeing to. He towered over Stephen by half a foot and made points with that, too. Finally, Stephen, voice soft but vibrant with prophecy, found the club with which to bully the bully. "Let harm

215

come to but one of those children, and the *Tribune* will have your hide. I'll see to that personally. It will become my mission." From then on things had improved.

The midway mark. More spectators now, bearing torches and lining both sides of Grand Street. He noticed Margaret noticing. She waited for him to reach her and then walked along at his side.

"They hate us," she said.

"Everyone hates everyone these days," he said. "It's in the air, like cholera."

She looked at him. She stopped and made him stop. He felt the strong grip of her fingers on his upper arm. "Please don't you hate me, Stephen. Even if you think you have a right to."

Effie called her away before he could answer, leaving him with the image of a pale, tight-lipped face. And words that struck at his heart. "Even if you think you have a right to." What in God's name did that mean? *Did* he have a right to? Did he only *think* he had a right to, a misconception that would prove banishable by pertinent explanations? Damn you, Margaret.

And now quite suddenly, while still a block short of the pier, the crowd was substantial. Two hundred or so, he thought, his stomach tightening. Catcalling, jeering, though not rock throwing. Not yet.

But they had cordoned off the pier. Not with ropes, with people. The entrance to the pier was through a brick passageway that stretched thirty feet across the water and rose ten feet under a wooden cover. In the neck of this stood about fifty or so, men mostly, a smattering of women. Shouting. Waving rudely lettered signs and banners. One of the more popular messages—it was triplicated—read: "Nigger babies today; nigger rapists tomorrow." Revulsion mastered fear. Stephen found himself coldly angry.

While the nurses did what they could to calm the children, the escort lined up in front of them—Sergeant Prendergast positioned at the head of his squad. Stephen moved up alongside. The huge sergeant glanced at him. It was the kind of glance to be expected from a policeman to a civilian, but something in Stephen's face must have made him acceptable. Without comment Prendergast

216

shifted a half step to the right, accommodating him. And then, for a while, they just listened:

"Drown the little bastards."

"Into the river with 'em. The only good nigger is a dead nigger."

And yet Stephen began to think they had no real heart for it. Bored and drunk, they were there because they were there—the mob its own reason for being. In an hour a new mobby rumor would be hatched causing a new mobby directive to be issued, and the crowd, like a giant balloon, would waft itself to another part of the city.

"Sergeant," Stephen said, loud enough to be heard across the twenty foot gulf that separated the two contingents, "do you see that large savage over there? The one in the scruffy red bandanna?"

Prendergast looked blank for a moment. Then, pointing with his locust stick, he said, "Aye, that's the one you mean, sir. The one making that infernal racket."

"Shoot him."

While the dialogue between the two was by no means loud it had sufficient flavor to capture attention. The crowd quieted. In the meantime the man in the red bandanna, singled out by Stephen on the assumption that he qualified, more or less, as one of the leaders, swung his own homemade club in the air like a scimitar, and demanded a parley.

"Do you want to parley with him, sir?" Prendergast asked.

"No. Shoot him."

"Now?"

"At three."

Prendergast nodded to his squad and they shouldered their weapons.

It was the signal for the crowd to divide. Though only half actually deserted, the remaining half did what it could short of that to cooperate in isolating the target.

"Where you going?" Red Bandanna demanded, bravado not quite enough to keep his voice absolutely steady. "They ain't going to shoot me. They—"

"One," Stephen said.

217

"Ain't nobody going to shoot nobody."

"Two," Stephen said, which was as far as it was necessary to go. The path to the pier was no longer defended.

"Nigger lover," the man in the red bandanna screamed in a furious valedictory, but from well up on Grand Street, and Stephen did not even look in his direction.

The ferry was in place. But the children filed on board under the sullen witnessing of her captain. Silent, ungracious, he watched as if the children were an invading horde. When the embarkation was complete, he approached Stephen and, after some preliminary grunting and snarling, demanded the rest of his money.

"The second third as agreed," Stephen said handing him an envelope. "The final third on Blackwell's. From Mrs. Singleton when she takes the children into her custody."

"How do I know this Mrs. Singleton will be waiting for them?"

"It's for taking small risks like that that you're being paid five times your usual fare."

"I want the rest now. Now, or the bloody ferry don't stir."

He held out his hand. Sergeant Prendergast arrived in time to crack it smartly with his stick.

"On Blackwell's," Stephen said.

Dennison skulked off.

Prendergast watched after him thoughtfully. "I think the squad and me will take ourselves a ferry ride. Would that be in order, Mr. Jardine?"

"It would assure the children a pleasanter crossing."

"Done, then."

Stephen turned for a last look at the array of small faces.

"Just babies," Prendergast said. "Just little babies, no matter what the color. You think them savages really meant to do them harm?"

"If it had got started wrong . . ." He refused to complete the thought even to himself.

"Bastards," Prendergast said bleakly.

The two men shook hands and parted. Once more back on the

pier, Stephen looked around for Margaret. He could not find her. Instead he found Jemima and Effie and learned from them that Margaret had gone home.

"She done good work for us," Jemima said. "She tired, deserves her rest." She spoke emphatically and stared at him hard-eyed as if he were the drainer of Margaret's strength.

He nodded and was moving away when Effie said, "Three days like we had . . ." She shook her head. "She so strong. She our inspiration."

"She the best leader we ever had," Jemima said.

"She like a soldier."

Stephen waited to see if more of this was to be aimed at him, but they were silent now. He bowed.

They gazed back at him unblinkingly.

He returned to Two hundred Mulberry Street to see if John had reappeared. He had not. Sergeant O'Neill guessed he might have gone searching for Michael. He waited half an hour or so, wandering aimlessly about, before deciding to go home. In no hurry to get there, he thought it predictable that a hack was waiting as if heaven-sent. He climbed in. He gave the driver his address. Heavily, he settled back against the leather.

She must have been watching for him, because she was at the open front door as he paid off the driver. He saw how nervous she was. She's guilty, he thought. Oh God, she's faithless, and now she's going to confess. He followed her into the drawing room, shutting the door. As she stared, stared, stared out the window he felt himself growing old. She did not stir. She was a tree. She would remain rooted there.

"I've sent him away," she said turning finally.

"What am I to understand from that?"

Her eyes widened. "I've never seen you so—"

"Margaret, have you been unfaithful to me?"

A change came over her. He knew that look. It was all Blanchard. "That will do, Stephen," she said icily. "You may go now. I will have a bag packed and sent to your club."

"Thank you," he said and turned instantly. He reached the door before she called his name. He stopped. No Blanchard now. She stood there, hands clasped penitently against her shirtwaist. She was shaking, tears streaming. His heart looped, and he ran back to crush her to him.

"I've written him, sending him away. Asking him never to come back. But we didn't, Stephen. Never. Not that I wasn't tempted. I was. I won't lie to you. It was because—"

"Enough. I've heard all that matters."

"Would you really have left me? Could you have?"

"I'd have tried."

"Oh God, I'll be better to you from now on. Oh, wait and see how good to you I'll be. As good as you deserve. Oh God, Stephen, I'd have turned my face to the wall."

He kissed her. She clung to him heavily, a dead weight, and yet he had not felt so light in days.

Not scented feathers, but her hair tickling his nose, he realized, coming out of the dream. He sniffed for more. How good it smelled. So clean, yes. And faintly perfumed. He wrapped a tendril around two of his fingers and pulled gently, thinking she might wake, hoping she would. But she did not. Just as well, he told himself sternly. He got out of bed, and, very quickly—so that he would not think better of it—began to dress. When he was finished, he went to the window and raised the shade. It was the noise of this that woke her.

"Come back here at once," she said.

"No. I can't."

"Instantly."

"Margaret, dearest, no. They need me at the *Tribune*."

"I need you here." Rising to her knees, she let the bed sheet slither shamelessly.

Defenceless against this, he was moving toward her when, out of the corner of his eye, he saw John Brautigan coming up the walk. One look told him something was wrong. He said as much to Margaret and hurried down the stairs. But when he opened the door Brautigan was smiling.

220

"Is Rosie here?" he asked.

"No. Margaret says she went to the armory looking for you. Come in, come in."

He continued to smile. Coming down the stairs, Margaret saw it, recognized it for the rictus it was and said, "Something's happened to Michael."

"Hello, Margaret," Brautigan said. "Your orphans reached Blackwell's safely. Prendergast—"

"Michael's hurt, isn't he?" Stephen said, cutting him off.

Again it was Margaret who guessed. Stephen, seeing it in her face, swung his glance back to Brautigan.

"Give him brandy," Margaret said and started back up the stairs.

"Where are you going?"

"To get dressed and find Rosie."

"How? She could be anywhere. If she's gone searching for John she could be at any one of eleven precincts."

"I'll find her," Margaret said grimly. "You attend to John."

Stephen took him into the drawing room and gave him the brandy Margaret had prescribed. He poured a glass for himself, too. Brautigan swallowed his instantly. And a second. It was when he was finishing the third that Stephen heard Margaret go out the front door.

In the years to come, nothing ever shook Stephen's conviction that the next hour was worse for him than it was for John. Because it seemed to him Brautigan had removed the essence of himself, taken a journey somewhere, leaving behind a husk to go through the motions of some macabre game, the object of which was to freeze time.

It was as if Michael were no more than away at school, his return imminently expected. In the next minute or so, that ancient maroon-and-gray Hamilton omnibus would be heard trundling over the cobblestones. John would shout down to Nora that their son was home and that she should please, for the love of heaven, open the door to him before he broke the screen for the dozenth time.

Comfortably sprawled in the deep leather armchair, downing

the brandies that had no appreciable effect on him, he told Stephen cheerful little stories about this trophy or that book, his voice never faltering.

"And you should have been there, Stephen. I mean to see that shell zip through the water, and Michael at cox, bellowing and berating . . . I mean you would have thought it was the Yalies against the Harvards. Of course next year he got his growth, and then he was too big to be in the shell at all."

Talking nonstop. Smiling, smiling, but with his eyes ready for pennies, Stephen thought. Had he passed his hand over them they would not have blinked.

At last he heard a carriage pulling up, then the clatter of hurrying footsteps. The front door was wrenched open. Rosie appeared in the doorway, Margaret a step behind.

As Rosie stood there a moment surveying, catching her breath, Brautigan smiled at her. It was the same awful smile Stephen had been witnessing for the better part of an hour. Seeing it, she crossed the room to him and shook him hard.

"Stop that. I won't stand for it, John."

By inches the smile faded. Seconds later the first wild sounds ripped out of him. Then the three helped each other to stretch him on the sofa.

"Leave them," Margaret said, taking Stephen's hand. "She knows what to do."

A last look showed him Rosie lying alongside Brautigan holding and caressing him, while sobbing shook that huge back like a baby's.

From Stephen Jardine's diary. Thursday, July 5.

. . . the eleventh, the sixty-fifth, and the seventy-fourth regiments reported on their way, the eleventh expected by morning. The riot is *in extremis.* By and large one walks quiet streets; sees open stores; flees not from strangers. Omnibuses and railroad cars are in full career again; ferries in full service. Peace tiptoes back among us. Tiptoes through puddles, for it has been raining most of the day. Rains then stops, rains and stops, as if the plan is to keep it flowing until the blood is washed away.

So much blood. We will never know the full extent of our casualties—in part because many of the rioters were buried secretly, at night, by clandestine parties carrying the bodies across the East River. In the mayor's office, I have heard estimates as high as a thousand. There they estimate property damage in the vicinity of a million and a half dollars.

Well, what brought it down on us? There are two great views. Greeley's and Bennett's. It goes without saying they are opposed.

Greeley (from today's editorial): "It was not simply a riot, but a piece of wickedness organized and perpetuated by the members of the Southern conspiracy and their Northern sympathizers."

Bennett's perspective is historical, and, it seems to me, nearer the mark. Prior to Fort Sumter, he points out, jobs were scarce, a situation that changed, improved, when war broke out. Now up from slavery comes the black man to discover that even a free belly requires food. He must eat. To eat he must work. To work he must compete. And so the black man becomes the Irish-American's rival. Inevitably his enemy, his *bête noire*, to echo Bennett's tasteless joke. And how often, he asks, are men eager to risk death for the sake of their *bêtes noires*?

Bennett says these were the conditions that made riot inescapable. Nor have we seen, he says, the last riot of its kind. Do I agree with *that*? I do not. He is a shameless old cynic. For seven days in a certain city, matches were put to tinder and riot happened. But our blacks will return from exile, and we will make amends to them. And the horror of this week will never be repeated. How could it be otherwise? Are we a race of Caligulas?

At the Union Club the talk is all of Terence Tyrell's murder. He was found in his own study—by Robbo Royce—with a knife plunged deep in his chest. A powerful man was behind that blow, an arm well known to the police, according to Sergeant O'Neil, who recognized the dagger instantly. The killer is a fierce old black named Frederick Berryman. Apparently, he left the weapon behind deliberately, as a signature. I ought neither to write it nor think or feel it, but I find no eagerness in me for Berryman to be brought to justice. He brought Tyrell to justice. That is justice enough for the time being. Please, future twigs of the Jardine tree, read the above with tolerance. Boss Tyrell was a despicable man.

Mary Haines has gone to Paris. She always wanted to, now she has. I will not miss her. That book was closed long ago. No, I will not miss her, but I shall never forget her.

John is feeling better, Rosie reports by runner. Thank God. So much raw pain. Father-and-son pain. Fills this father with foreboding. What agony does young Stephen have in store for me?

A coward's thought if ever there was one.

A man loves his son and takes his chances, and that is the beginning and end of paterfamilias wisdom.

Went to a wedding yesterday—as part of the orphanage contingent—and saw Cora Dawson marry her lieutenant. Handsome couple—she, in particular, radiant. But even he seemed on the sunny side, a rare side for him. He is an admirable man, no doubt. Accomplished, dedicated . . . But—I confess it here—I never met anyone with a chillier smile. Not yesterday, though.

No news of Peter, no reply to Margaret's note to him. We speculate he may well be on his way to Washington. Will I ever see him again? The truth is I am not eager to. Still, wounds heal. Perhaps in a year or two. Yes, let him return in a year or so.

In the meantime it is very sweet between the Jardines. And Margaret is calling now. . . .